DANGERZONE BOOKS PRESENTS

DANGER REALLY IS EVERYWHERE

SCHOOL OF DANGER

by Docter Noel Zone

'THE GREATEST DANGEROLOGIST
IN THE WORLD, EVER'

DANGER IS EVERYWHERE

D0228537

This book is dedicated to Gretel, my wonderful next-door neighbour and seller of the most delicious cabbages on earth.

I'm sorry for all the times I have shouted at your cat, Ethel, because I thought she was a baby tiger.

And I'm sorry for chopping your garden hose in half. It looked like a snake.

Also, I'm sorry for knocking over the hedge you had spent months trimming to look like a huge hen. I thought it was a huge hen and it was coming to peck you or lay an egg on you.

Same with your statue of an eagle that I broke with a patio chair.

And the snowman that I melted with your barbecue. And then accidentally set fire to the shed where you store your cabbages.

And I'm sorry for not being able to put out the burning shed and flaming cabbages because of the chopped hose.

Especially when the fire spread to the ruined hen hedge and then nearly set fire to Ethel.

OH, GRETEL,
I'M SO SORRY FOR ALL OF THESE THINGS!

I just don't want anything bad to happen to you because

DANGER REALLY IS EVERYWHERE.

Docter Noel Zone

Docter Noel Zone

(The Greatest Dangerologist in the World, **EVER**)

NOTE: Please know that I'm saving up to buy you a new shed.

NOTE 2: I am a DoctEr of **DANGEROLOGY**, not a DoctOr you'd find in a hospital or university.
People sometimes say the two words sound similar, but I have no idea how you could possibly mix them up.

NOW, LET'S BEGIN!

No, wait. # STOP!

Please put this book down and walk away. Just forget you ever saw it.

I'm afraid you are **NOT** allowed to read it. *

*UNLESS YOU CAN PASS THE FOLLOWING TEST.

You see, this is a book about **DANGEROLOGY.**

And **DANGEROLOGY** is the study of **DANGER** and how to avoid it. If you study **DANGEROLOGY** you are a **DANGEROLOGIST.**

NOTE: I know this because I invented the words

DANGEROLOGY and **DANGEROLOGIST.**

BUT with a book like this there's a risk that **REALLY, REALLY DANGEROUS INDIVIDUALS** could read it and learn **HOW TO BECOME EVEN MORE DANGEROUS.**

A DANGEROUS VIKING

For example, a **VAMPIRE** could discover my tricks
for spotting vampires.

1. They have **VERY** loud vampire farts (that go **HOOOOOONK**

2. These days, most vampires travel around by **SEGWAY**.

HOOOOOONK!!

And, having read this, that vampire might stop riding around on a
Segway and doing as many farts, and become

EVEN MORE DIFFICULT TO SPOT

and so be

EVEN MORE DANGEROUS.

In order to make sure that **YOU** are not going to use the **III** (Incredibly Important Information) contained in this book to cause **EVEN MORE DANGER,** we will begin with the

DROST

(Dangerology Reader Opening Suitability Test).

NOTE: In **DANGEROLOGY** we use **A LOT** of abbreviations because

ISALOTAYCUTTTMSNDIHAY

(It Saves A Lot Of Time And You Can Use That Time To Make Sure Nothing Dangerous Is Happening Around You).

There are four parts to the **DROST.** If you fail **ANY**
part, you may **NOT** read this book. **NO WAY.** You can't
even touch it. Or be in the same room as it. And don't
think you will get away with sneakily reading it.

I know where **ALL** the copies of this book are, and

I **REGULARLY** check up on who is reading them. If I

catch you, **YOU WILL BE IN BIG TROUBLE.**

Thank you.

DROST PART 1

CAN YOU PICK UP THIS BOOK, PLACE IT ON TOP OF YOUR HEAD AND BALANCE IT THERE FOR THREE SECONDS?

If you can, then you may read on.

If you can't, and it falls straight through you and lands **SPLAT** on the ground where your feet should be, then **GET AWAY FROM THIS BOOK BECAUSE YOU ARE A GHOST.**

Why don't you go off and read something that is meant for ghosts? Maybe a book called 'Hooowww to Improooove Yooour Wooooing' or '50 Faaaamous Waaalls to Goooooo Throoough Befooore the Aaaage of Fiiiive Huuuundred'.

FLOAT OFF, YOU BIG, ANNOYING, STINKY CLOUD.

NOTE: Ghosts smell like the inside of very old shoes.

NOTE 2: This book is NOT for ghosts. **IT'S FOR LEVEL 3 PODs.**

NOTE 3: By starting this book, you have become a Level 3 **POD** (**P**upil **O**f **D**angerology).

CONGRATULATIONS!

NOTE 4: If you finish it, you will be a Level 3 **FOD** (**F**ull-**O**n **D**angerologist).

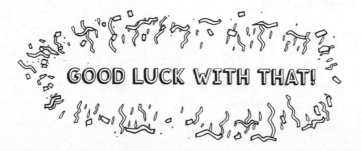

GOOD LUCK WITH THAT!

DROST PART 2

Close this book and toss it **VERY CAREFULLY AND GENTLY** on to a cushion or mattress across the room. Now, did you feel the urge to run after it, pick it up with your huge claws or big dribbly teeth and then bring it back to the spot where you threw it from, like a dog/wolf?

Is your entire body covered in thick fur and, instead of talking, do you go '**RARR, RARR, RARR**', love being tickled and sometimes (when there is a full moon) eat people who are out jogging?

If you answered **YES** to **ANY** of these questions, **THEN YOU MAY NOT READ THIS BOOK BECAUSE YOU ARE A WEREWOLF.**

NOTE: If you are a werewolf, I suggest you go off and live in a cave or a forest that is **VERY FAR AWAY** from here, and that hopefully already has a grumpy bear living in it who will **NOT BE AT ALL HAPPY** with a new housemate.

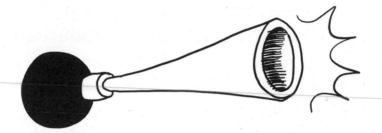

HONK!

HONK!

WAIT!

That honking is the sound of the **RAD** (**R**eally **A**wfully **D**angerous) **HORN**, which tells us that something **REALLY AWFULLY DANGEROUS** is coming up.

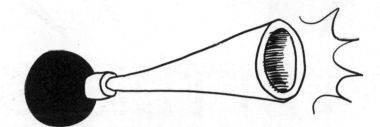

NOTE: It is important not to confuse the sound of the **RAD HORN** with the sound of a vampire fart. The **RAD HORN** goes **HONK! HONK!** whereas the vampire fart goes **HOOOONNNNK.**

HONK! HONK!

The **RAD HORN** is honking because it's time for a

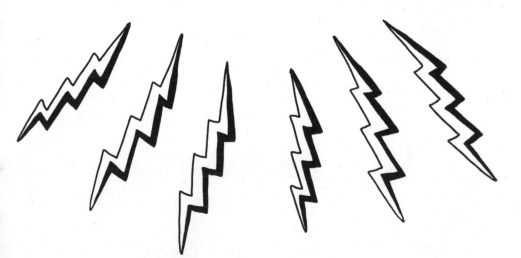

VSITTDROST

(Very Serious Interruption To The DROST).

Experienced **DANGEROLOGISTS** will be aware of my war with the **PAGE 9 SCORPION.** This is a devious bug that lives in bookshops and libraries, and likes to sneak into books and lie in wait on page 9.

Then when anyone opens page 9 it jumps out and attaches itself to their nose, firing poison from its creepy-crawly botty.

To avoid these attacks, you will notice that there is no page 9 in this book. I have cunningly renamed it

page **NOEL**.

NOEL

In fact, to be **EXTRA SAFE,** from this point on, whenever there is a number 9 in this book, I will change it to the word **NOEL.** So, for example, the page after page 18 will be page **NOEL**teen, and the page before 100 will be page **NOELTY-NOEL.** This should be enough to confuse the **PAGE NOEL SCORPION** and save you from any nose injuries.

YOU
ARE
WELCOME.

Sorry, back to the **DROST.**

DROST PART 3

Take a moment to look at your hands holding this book. **ARE THEY COVERED IN WHITE BANDAGES?** Now check your face in the mirror. **IS IT COVERED IN WHITE BANDAGES TOO?** Look down. **ARE YOU COVERED ENTIRELY IN WHITE BANDAGES?**

If you answered yes to any of these questions, then you may **NOT** read any more of this book, because it means you are an **ANCIENT EGYPTIAN MUMMY** that has come back to life, and they are **ALWAYS** angry and up to bad stuff. I mean, when was the last time you heard a story of an ancient Egyptian mummy doing anything good?

'Oh, my bike got a flat tyre, but then a **MUMMY** ran out of the bushes and fixed it.'

ANSWER = NEVER + EVER

NOTE: This is a bad example because CYCLING IS VERY DANGEROUS, and I do not recommend that you ever do it.

NOTE 2: Can I just be clear that when I say a 'MUMMY' can't read this book, I mean an **ANCIENT EGYPTIAN MUMMY.** Mothers and grandmothers are very welcome to continue reading.

NOTE 3: Hang on. Not if your mother is a **MUMMY.** In that case, you can read it, but she can't.

NOTE 4: If you are covered in bandages because you have recently been in an accident, then you may continue to the final part of the **DROST.**

NOTE 5: If **NOTE 4** applies to you, then I am very sorry. I didn't mean to compare you to an ancient Egyptian mummy. Also, **GET WELL SOON.**

DROST PART 4

CAN YOU PUT THIS WHOLE BOOK INSIDE YOUR MOUTH AND THEN CLOSE YOUR MOUTH SO THAT NOBODY WOULD KNOW YOU'VE GOT A BOOK IN YOUR MOUTH?

If you can't, and it sticks out like a big paper flapjack, then you may read on, because it means

YOU ARE NOT A GIANT.

But if you can easily fit it in, then **PLEASE SPIT IT OUT AND GO BACK UP YOUR BEANSTALK OR MOUNTAIN OR WHEREVER GIANTS LIVE AND NEVER COME NEAR ME OR THIS BOOK AGAIN.**

NOT A GIANT

If you are still reading now, then

You have passed the **DROST** and **YOU MAY CONTINUE** with the rest of this book.

 **Thank you.**

NOTE: I love to give things a thumbs-up. However, a thumb stuck straight up is too pointy! So I have developed this

ultra-safe thumbs-up-and-then-down-a-bit or **TUATDAB.** It provides all of the encouragement of the old thumbs-up with none of the poking danger.

Now put on your

DANGER HELMET,

don your

T-COD

(Tiny Cape Of Dangerology)

and get ready to toot your

DAD

(Danger Alerting Device),

because this is **NOT** the sort of book
that gently eases you into the action.

NO WAY.

We are going straight out on

DANGER
PATROL.

WHAT IS DANGER PATROL?

A superb question there from you! **GOOD WORK**, Level 3 **POD!**
You are **REALLY** paying attention.

This book will teach you about **DANGEROLOGY**
by giving you a glimpse into a week in the
INCREDIBLY EXCITING LIFE (see pictures below)
of the **WORLD'S LEADING DANGEROLOGIST** (me).

9 a.m. walk pet stone

1 p.m. drink tea (cold)

3 p.m. mow the grass
NOTE: Blades have been removed, so it's really 'squash the grass'.

And a vital part of Level 3 **DANGEROLOGY** is being
aware of any **NEW DANGERS** that could be in your area.
The best way to do this is by carrying out regular and
thorough **DANGER PATROLS.**

VERY IMPORTANT! VERY IMPORTANT!

PREPARATIONS BEFORE YOU GO OUT ON DANGER PATROL

1. Put on your **FULL DANGEROLOGY UNIFORM.** This is vital for working in **DANGEROUS CONDITIONS,** such as **INDOORS** or, in this case, **OUTDOORS.**

2. As we will be **DANGEROLOGING** on the street, remember to wear a **REFLECTIVE VEST** and one of the following **EXTRA-HIGH-VISIBILITY** accessories:

-Christmas tinsel and fairy lights

-a helmet made of a glitter ball

-a **HELMET CONE**

NOTE: Today I have opted for this stylish **HELMET CONE.**

3. Remember to bring a **PORB**

PORB

(**P**ortable **O**bservation **R**ecording **B**ooklet)
to take note of any **DANGERS** you encounter. As all books
(INCLUDING THIS ONE YOU ARE HOLDING) have
SHARP CORNERS (I HOPE YOU ARE WEARING YOUR
PROTECTIVE READING GLOVES), I advise keeping your
PORB inside a soft travel case.
Examples of safe travel cases include:

in between two sponges

inside a baby's nappy (**MAKE SURE**
IT'S A FRESH ONE)

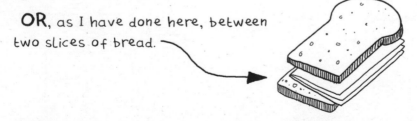

OR, as I have done here, between
two slices of bread.

NOTE: DO NOT TRY TO EAT IT WHEN YOU ARE HUNGRY.

A PORB sandwich is **NAAD** (**N**ot **A**t **A**ll **D**elicious).

22

4. If possible, bring a

DASK

(DANGEROLOGY Assisting Side-Kick)

along with you, to help spot danger, or save you if anything **RAD** (Really Awfully Dangerous) happens.

A NOTE ON MY NEW DASK:

I had asked my nieces, Katherine and Millicent, to call in after school today, but unfortunately — and this happens quite often when I ask them to help me — they were busy. Katherine said she had to melt some ice cubes, and Millicent was washing her toothbrush.

So instead they sent their little brother, **TEDDY**.

Now, Teddy has been telling me for a **LONG TIME** that he is old enough to become a **DANGEROLOGIST**, but today he made the **WORST POSSIBLE ARRIVAL** by turning up in **THE MOST DANGEROUS WAY**: on his **BICYCLE**.

HONK! HONK!

I have pointed out to him **MANY TIMES** how **DANGEROUS BICYCLES ARE**, but he really loves that thing. He even has a special blanket that he puts over it when it's time for bed.

NOTE: He calls his bike Liam.

Teddy may not immediately strike you as the perfect **DASK** — he does tend to worry a lot and can panic when unexpected things happen, but he is **HIGHLY** enthusiastic and eager to learn. He is also very good at pushing a **DORK**.

WHAT IS A DORK, DOCTER NOEL?

ANOTHER EXCELLENT QUESTION. The best way to take notes in your **PORB** while on the move is with a **DORK**, or

Danger **O**bservation **R**econnaissance **K**art.

It is a **MOBILE DANGEROLOGY OFFICE.**

You could use a **WHEELIE BIN**

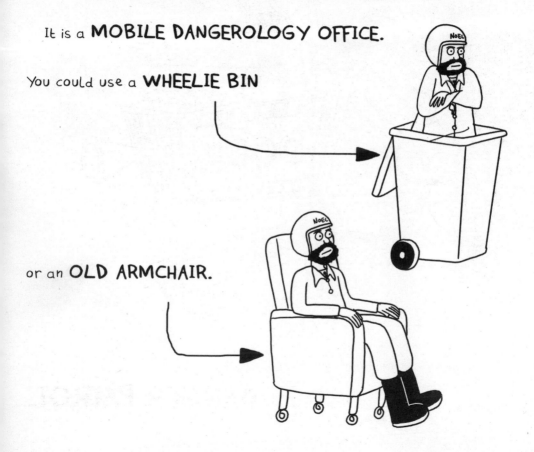

or an **OLD ARMCHAIR.**

I have adapted a **SUPERMARKET TROLLEY** I got from the scrap yard

Now, wish us luck as we head off on **DANGER PATROL**.

Well, Level 3 **PODs**, that didn't go **EXACTLY** as expected.

It started **VERY WELL.** We trundled off towards the supermarket and **IMMEDIATELY** I began to take great notes in my **PORB.**

DANGER PATROL OBSERVATION 1:

NEW TRAFFIC LIGHTS OUTSIDE THE SUPERMARKET

Traffic Lights give me such different feelings,
depending on which colour they are.

When they are orange and all of that dreadful traffic slows down, I think, 'This isn't so bad. I quite like traffic lights.'

And then when they go red and the traffic stops completely

I think, 'Traffic lights are **THE BEST**!' I imagine how great it would be if they were like this all the time. No whooshy cars, no beepy horns. For a moment, everything is calm in the world.

But then they change to their third colour, and in an instant
EVERYTHING IS RUINED.

TWENTY-NOEL

I feel **VERY** strongly about this. And, when I feel very strongly about something, it can inspire one of my very powerful poems. I call this one simply:

GREEN

by Docter Noel Zone

O Green, you can be so beautiful,
Cabbages always make me smile.
But you are also the colour of aliens,

AND DANGEROUS TREES

AND HUNGRY CROCODILES

AAAAGH TRAFFIC LIGHTS, NOOOO,

AAAAGH, AAAAGH, NOOOO, NOOOO.

I think you'll agree it got quite emotional towards the end of that poem. Please take a moment to dry your tears if you are crying.

NOTE: BE CAREFUL NOT TO CREATE A SLIPPY TEAR PUDDLE.

Thank you.

Dangerologists should never be afraid to face **DANGER**, but Teddy had a fair point here.

'Good thinking, nephew!' I said. 'Now, let's continue the **DANGER PATROL.**'

DANGER PATROL OBSERVATION 2: THE BMX GANG

As Teddy pushed me past the big gates of the school, the four older kids, who always hang out there were sitting on their BMX bikes.

As usual, they were **NOT** being very positive about my **DANGEROLOGY,** so I decided to make a note of them in my **PORB.**

'UH-OH, WEIRDY BEARDY ALERT,'
said Sunglasses.

'Here comes Helmet Head!' yelled Hood.

'Look, it's Docter Noel Cone!' added Hat.

'Very nice boots,' said Spike, and they all
looked at him.

'What?' he said. 'I like his boots.'

'You are supposed to say something
mean!' said Sunglasses.

'Oh yeah. Sorry, I forgot.' Spike looked
down at his shoes. He isn't the smartest
member of the gang.

'Wait, look! He's got a mini cone-panion!'
said Sunglasses, pointing at Teddy pushing

the **DORK.**

'That's Teddy from Class One!' Hood said.

'Hi, g-g-guys.' Teddy didn't seem very excited that
they had recognized him. 'We're actually p-p-pretty
busy at the moment.'

'Teddy, if you just bought him in the supermarket,
you should ask for your money back!' said Hat.

'Teddy's got nice boots too,' said Spike, and they
all looked at him again.

'WE'RE SUPPOSED TO BE ZINGING THEM,'
shouted Sunglasses.

Something like this happens every time I pass the school,
but Teddy wasn't used to it.

'GUYS, WE ARE T-T-TRYING TO DO SOME REALLY IMPORTANT D-D-DANGEROLOGY WORK HERE!'
he yelled.

They all laughed at him.

'Yes, taking your giant baby for a walk is really important, Teddy!' said Sunglasses.

'I think your son may be a bit big for his pram,' said Hood.

'And he's such a hairy baby!' added Hat.

'Good job pushing it, Teddy. It looks heavy,' said Spike, and they all shouted at him again.

'We'd love to stay and chat, but we have important **DANGEROLOGY** to get on with,' I said, and Teddy pushed me up the road.

DANGER PATROL OBSERVATION 3:
WHIZZY THINGS OUTSIDE THE SCHOOL

What I did notice around the school was the number

of students **WHIZZING** past me on their small

whizzy vehicles. You already know how I feel

about bicycles, but there were also:

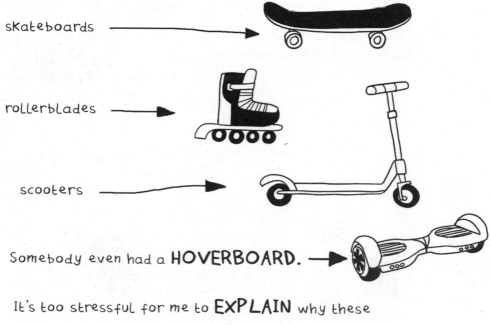

skateboards

rollerblades

scooters

Somebody even had a **HOVERBOARD.**

It's too stressful for me to **EXPLAIN** why these

objects **ARE ALL INCREDIBLY DANGEROUS** so I will

show you with a diagram.

HONK! HONK!

But it would be **SO EASY** to make them all **100% SAFE**.

HOW I WOULD MAKE ALL OF THESE THINGS
100% SAFE:

Step one: Remove the wheels.

THAT'S IT. Without wheels, suddenly they can all be used for other, less dangerous things.

Rollerblades become **CLOMPY BOOTS**, useful for walking very slowly — the safest kind of walking.

A skateboard becomes **A PIECE OF WOOD**, which you can use as a shelf for your **PORB**s or **AN IRONING BOARD** for your **DANGER-ONESIE.**

A scooter without its wheels can be used as a weather vane. Or attach two skateboards to a scooter and you have **AN UMBRELLA. EVEN MORE USEFUL!**

Remove the wheels from a hoverboard, place it beside your front door and you have a

BOOT-SCRAPER.

Ideal for removing mud from the bottom of your shoes

and **CLOMPY BOOTS.**

And a bicycle without its wheels is a **USELESS PILE OF JUNK**, and that is **ONE MILLION TIMES** better **AND** safer than a bicycle.

At least then it can be **RECYCLED** and made into something safer,

such as an exercise bike, a **DORK** or **A DANGER WARNING SIGN.**

DON'T CYCLE. RECYCLE!

THIRTY-NOEL

DANGER PATROL OBSERVATION 4:
NEW TREES BY THE TRAIN STATION

I CAN'T BELIEVE I WASN'T CONSULTED ABOUT THESE,
because I would have staged a protest. I'd have
lain on the ground so they couldn't be planted.

Not only do trees attract **UNBELIEVABLY DANGEROUS**

THINGS, such as **LIGHTNING, KITES** and **TREE HOUSES,**
but at any moment a branch could fall off and

donk you on the **DANGER HELMET.**

Trees can also be home to **INCREDIBLY DANGEROUS ANIMALS.** We will now look at some of the most awful ones in a special

AAAAaAAA

(Advice About Avoiding Angry and Aggressive Animal Attacks)

focusing on

BEASTS of the TREES

1. GRAB-BEES

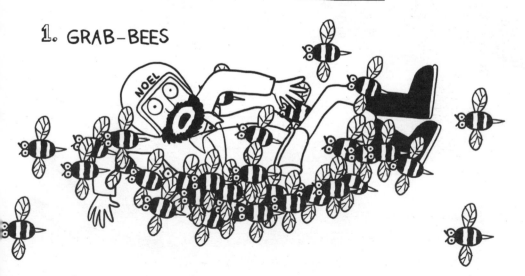

You'd better like the taste of honey because where these bees are taking you **IT'S THE ONLY THING TO EAT.**

2. GLUE-POOP PIGEONS

Sit on one of their poops, and you'll be staying on that park bench for some time. And if it lands in your hair **YOU'LL HAVE TO CHOP IT ALL OFF.**

3. THE WEDGIE GIBBON

Their long arms reach down from trees/hedges and pull your undies up **MUCH** higher than they are supposed to go.

4. SNATCHY SQUIRRELS

It's not just that they come down and steal your wallet, it's that they **THEN** use your bank card to buy things online.

'I don't remember ordering **NOEL** tons of nuts?' 'When did I buy this mini tree-hammock and bushy-tail hairdryer?'

5. ALLEAFGATOR

When **LEAVES** fall off, they become **MINI DANGER-CARPETS** and offer the perfect hiding place for some real nasties — the worst of which is the dreaded **ALLEAFGATOR.** This is a frightening reptile (from Belgium) that preys on people who enjoy kicking piles of leaves. One encounter with an **ALLEAFGATOR** and you will **NEVER** look forward to autumn again.

I spend **A LOT** of my time catching leaves that fall into **THE DANGERGARDEN** (**NOTE:** this is what I call my garden) from the messy giraffes that live over the wall, in the giraffe enclosure of the zoo.

This used to be **ANNOYING** as the giraffes are **ALWAYS** chewing and staring, chewing and staring.

But recently it has become **REALLY, REALLY ANNOYING.**

You see, there's a new giraffe. And it's not just
the extra chewing and staring — and he does

A LOT of that. With this one, it's something

MUCH WORSE. It's the name the idiot zookeepers
have given him.

They've called him **NOEL.**

45

So now, at least once a day, I hear somebody calling **MY** name and rush out to **THE DANGERGARDEN** to see if there has been a **DANGERMERGENCY.**

But what I find isn't a person in **SERIOUS DANGER.**

Instead, it's a grinning, drooling baby giraffe with a tongue as long as a football sock, who — and this is the worst part — is always so happy to see me.

He thinks I am his best friend.

LEAVE ME ALONE, GIRAFFE. I'M THE MAIN NOEL AROUND HERE.

Also,

YOU *LOOK* LIKE A PONY THAT HAS SWALLOWED A ROLL OF CARPET.

Sorry, I got sidetracked there.

Back to today's **DANGER PATROL REPORT**.

For the final part of our mission, we were patrolling on the hill by the shopping centre.

And this is where things started to go **BADLY** wrong.

Teddy made the same basic **DANGEROLOGY MISTAKE** I made when I smashed Gretel's cement eagle with her patio chair. He thought that the statue of the dog by the shopping centre **WAS A REAL DOG**.

And that it was coming for us.

'Uncle N-N-Noel! It's **A H-H-HUGE D-D-DOGGY!**'

Just for a second, he took his hands off the **DORK**,
and that was all it took to start rolling down the hill.

HONK! HONK! HONK!

TOOT! TOOT! TOOT!

I furiously honked the **RAD HORN** on the front of the
DORK, while tooting my **DAD**.

> **NOTE:** In Level 3 **DANGEROLOGY,** three
> **TOOTS** means: **'PLEASE HELP ME.'**

'**TEDDY! TEDDY!**' But, by the time he realized the
statue was only a statue, I had built up quite a
bit of speed.

The hill took the **DORK** straight into the busy shopping centre. **'PARDON ME!'** I yelled as I sped through the entrance, and then suddenly

DUGGA-DUGGA-DUGGA-DUGGA

I was bumping down the escalator as shoppers with big bags dived out of the way.

'SORRY ABOUT THIS!' I shouted as toilet rolls and cartons of milk went everywhere.

With Teddy in hot pursuit, I rolled out of the back entrance of the shopping centre and started freewheeling down the wrong side of the main road.

FORTY-NOEL

Steering and braking are impossible in a runaway **DORK**, so cars and buses were swerving to avoid me. The policewoman saw me pass by and jumped on her motorbike.

The BMX gang by the school gates were very surprised to see me again, this time going at a much higher speed — with Teddy and the policewoman following behind.

I was relieved to see the big hedge at the bottom of the street. It could have been something much less squashy. But, just as I prepared for a hedgy impact, a pedestrian stepped directly into the path of the **DORK.**

She was wearing big red headphones. I yelled, honked and tooted as loud as I could, but she didn't hear a thing.

The **DORK** slammed into the edge of the path at the bottom of the road and I shot out.

By the time Teddy pulled me out of the hedge, the policewoman had helped the lady to sit up.

'I'm so sorry,' I said to them both. 'I lost control.'

Jane the policewoman was furious.

'Do you realize how many laws you have just broken? Driving an uninsured vehicle without due care and

attention **THROUGH A SHOPPING CENTRE**? And then the wrong way — through traffic lights — down a busy road. Not to mention the damage to this hedge. If this pedestrian hadn't jumped out of the way, it

could have been **SO** much worse!'

'Oh dear,' I said to the lady with the headphones. 'Are you OK?'

'I think I am. I landed on my shoulder. It's sore, but nothing feels broken,' she said, smiling bravely.

'Hello, Chloe!' said Teddy.

'Oh, you two know each other? I'm Docter Noel Zone.' I held out my hand, then realized that she couldn't reach out to shake it.

'Well, if you're a doctor,' said Jane the policewoman, 'maybe you should be helping this woman.'

'Oh, I didn't say "doctor". I said "**DOCTER**". I'm a **DOCTER OF DANGEROL—**'

But the policewoman had stopped listening. 'Chloe, if you want to press charges, I can arrest this doctor — or whatever he is — for public endangerment.'

'**WHAT?**' I said.

'If Chloe wants, I will arrest you and take you down to the station.'

'N-no,' I spluttered. 'The other part.'

'Public endangerment. It means you were being **DANGEROUS.**'

The word echoed around my head.

Nobody had **EVER** called me that before. And it felt **WORSE THAN THE WORST NIGHTMARE I'VE EVER HAD.**

NOTE: here is a scene from the worst nightmare I've ever had.

'Don't worry. I won't be pressing any charges,'
said Chloe. 'It was nobody's fault. Probably just an
accident while you and Teddy were shopping.'

'Thank you! Thank you so much,' I said. 'If there's
anything I can do to make it up to you, let me know.'

'Well, I don't think I'm going to be able to go back
to work for a while,' Chloe said.

'Let me fill in at your job till you're better!'

'Are you sure?' she said.

'Of course! It's the very least I can do.'

'Ok then! Just make sure you're there at quarter to nine
tomorrow and that you have three hundred school lunches
    ready for twelve thirty.'

'Chloe is the chef in the c-c-canteen at school,' said Teddy.

I had not expected that, but, then again, it had been
a highly unpredictable afternoon, generally.

'You are about to see a lot more of me,' I said to my nephew as we pushed the battered **DORK** back towards THE DANGERZONE.

'DOCTER NOEL ZONE IS GOING BACK TO SCHOOL!'

OK, so I don't know much about being a chef.

But I know **A HUGE AMOUNT** about **DANGER.** So, before I begin this job tomorrow morning, here are my

TTTFADIES

(Top Ten Tips For Avoiding Danger In Everyday Situations)

in one of the most **DANGEROUS** places of all:

DANGER
AT
SCHOOL

1. RUSHING AROUND

The most common cause of **ACCIDENTS** at school is people **DASHING ABOUT THE PLACE.** Eliminate this risk by insisting that everyone wears **VERY SLOW FOOTWEAR.** For example, **SNOWSHOES, HAY BALES** or **VELCRO SOLES.**

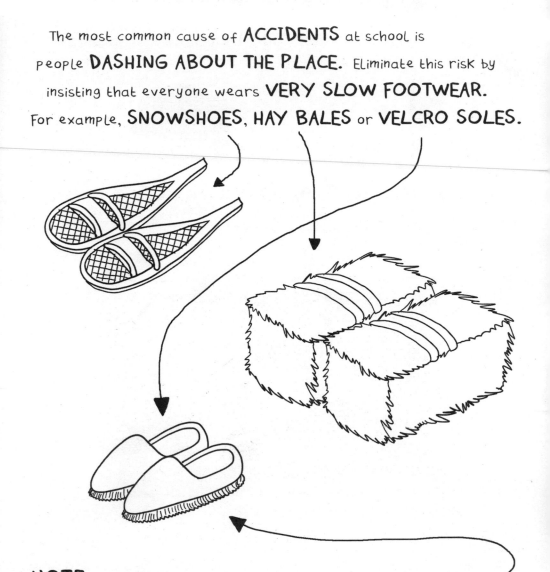

NOTE: This one only works if you have hairy school carpets.

FIFTY-NOEL

2. SCHOOL UNIFORMS

AWFUL SCHOOL UNIFORM DANGERS are waiting to happen every day.

Instead, all students should wear
protective headwear, along with sturdy boots,
a full-length onesie, and why not finish off the look with a

handy (and stylish) **PEBB** (**P**ersonal **E**mergency **B**um **B**ag)?

NOTE: Correct. Everyone should dress like me.

3. SNEAKY SCHOOL BEASTS

Devious animals could be hiding in your school, waiting to chomp you.

Beware of the **RULER ANACONDA,**

the **PAINTBRUSH PYTHON**

and the **STAPLER GECKO.**

4. THE SCHOOL LIBRARY

Not only home to the dreaded **PAGE NOEL SCORPION**,
the school library can also be the location of
MANY OTHER AWFUL DANGERS, such as:

BOOKVALANCHES (also known as **BOOKSHELF BARFS**)

LADDER FLOPS

BOOK-TROLLEY CRASHES

VAMPIRE LIBRARIANS
(**VAMPIRES** love to eat paper and are
often found where there is a lot of it.)

5. SCHOOL CHAIRS

These are **MUCH** too dangerous, as daydreaming students can easily topple off them. **ALL** chairs should be replaced with **BEANBAGS.**

Desks are dangerous too, and they should also be replaced with **BIGGER BEANBAGS.**

WARNING: Before you sit on **ANY** beanbag, make sure **IT IS A BEANBAG,** and not a **SEA LION** that has wandered into your school by mistake and is trying to have a snooze.

6. NEW STUDENTS

Before welcoming any new students to school, make sure they **DEFINITELY ARE STUDENTS** and not **DANGEROUS ANIMALS IN DISGUISE** trying to sneak into your school **TO CHOMP EVERYONE.**

Some giveaways include:

-very large teeth or beaks,

-saying their name is **GRRRRRR** or **RARR.**

-Also do they eat their lunch with their face directly in the food while making this sound: **NOMF-NOMF-NOMF?**

-Do they have a big fin on their back and spend all of their time in a big tank of water?

7. SCHOOL BAGS

These are heavy and can hurt your back.

Much safer is a **BOOK-BARROW,**

a **COAT-LIBRARY** or a **TEXTBOOK TAIL.**

8. SCHOOL BREAK TIME

This is another **INCREDIBLY DANGEROUS TIME OF DAY.**

Avoid playground accidents by making sure you never go outside. Use a hose to turn **BREAK TIME** into **RAIN TIME** so everyone has to stay in.

NOEL. SCHOOL TRIPS AND EXCURSIONS

Too often, school trips are to **INCREDIBLY DANGEROUS LOCATIONS**, such as **CASTLES**, **MUSEUMS** and even **ADVENTURE PARKS**. How about going somewhere much safer and more enjoyable? Such as:

- a cushion/mattress shop

- a bubble-wrap factory

- or a cabbage shop (I suggest Gretel's Cabbage Cabin).

Why not just stay in the school and **IMAGINE** you have gone on a school trip while sitting on your beanbag and looking at the rain.

10. SCHOOL SPORTS

WHY WOULD YOU WANT TO RUN AROUND IN THE COLD, CHASING A BALL OF SOME KIND, OFTEN WHILE HOLDING A DANGEROUS STICK?

No way. **NO WAY.**

The only thing I like about sport is **THE SAFETY EQUIPMENT.** So, if you really must play, remember to wear **ALL OF IT** regardless of what sport you are playing. That includes:

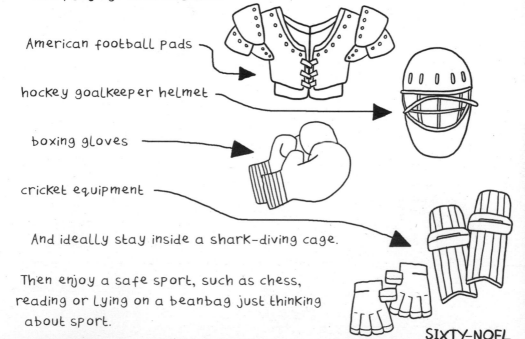

American football pads

hockey goalkeeper helmet

boxing gloves

cricket equipment

And ideally stay inside a shark-diving cage.

Then enjoy a safe sport, such as chess, reading or lying on a beanbag just thinking about sport.

SIXTY-NOEL

The school is a big grey box with a dull-green beard of ivy trying to grow up it. Above the main door is the school motto:

**PLEASE TRY
REALLY HARD.**

Inside, long corridors are lined with old class photographs, broken up by doors to different classrooms and offices.

Teddy spotted me arriving and led me straight to the assembly hall, where a lampposty-shaped man with a moustache like a neatly groomed croissant was pacing back and forth impatiently on the stage

'Hullo, stuuudents and staaaff.'

This was Mr Staples, the headmaster.
Sometimes known as 'Springy' Staples,
because he could pop up anywhere.
More often known as

  'the

      most

         boring

           man

             in

               the

                 world'.

'If I can just haaave your attention,'
he began, and already I found it hard not to
drift off. I noticed the BMX gang chatting to
each other in the back row, ignoring
Staples as he droned on.

'I'm sooorry to start the day with something
sooo serioooous but I dooon't know how else
to break it tooo you . . . A bicycle was
stolen from the schoool last night.
Madeleine left it heeere, and this
morning it's gone.'

There was total **SILENCE** in the hall, except for the faint weeping of Madeleine.

'If anyone noootices anything suspicious around school or knooows anything, pleeease let me know.'

NOTE: As Staples is not a **DANGEROLOGIST**, he did not know how much safer his student was without her awful bicycle. I made a note in my **PORB** to tell him after assembly.

But the audience was still in shock. Mr Staples tried to move on to other announcements.

'Also, I hope everyone is traaaining for the school sports day which begins at ten a.m. sharp on Satur—'

'W-w-wait,' said Teddy, standing up beside me. 'Is Madeleine's bike g-g-gone gone? As in, **GONE?**'

'Yes. I'm aaafraid so,' Springy replied.

Around me, everyone was shaking their heads in disbelief. This was big news.

'Finally we welcooome a new member of staaaff: our temporary school chef, Mr Zooone.'

I felt it was my duty as a **DANGEROLOGIST** to correct Mr Staples here.

'Excuse me,' I called out from the back of the room. 'It's actually **DOCTER** Noel Zone.'

'Doctor Dingbat, more like,' shouted Sunglasses, and the other members of the BMX gang burst out laughing.

But Mr Staples ignored them. 'Please excuuuse me.
I had nooo idea that you were a doctor. Perhaaaps
  you can give us a tour of your hospitaaal some time.'

'Well, no — see, I'm a **DOCTER** of **DANGEROL—**'

DING-A-LING-A-LING-A-LING!

The bell for the start of school rang before I had a chance
to correct his mistake.

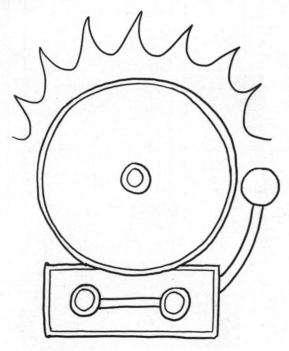

As the students rushed off to their
classrooms, I went to find the school kitchen,
pushing the wheelbarrow of cookbooks
I had borrowed from Gretel.

THE SCHOOL KITCHEN

Chef Chloe had left a very nice note stuck to the front of the enormous fridge.

WELCOME, NOEL!

Sorry if my writing is a bit wobbly. I called in after the hospital and my arm is in a sling.

Thank you SO MUCH for taking over. The nurse says I can come back to work next Monday, so just follow my plan for the rest of the week, or make up your own!

Good luck!

Chef Chloe

The chalkboard with Chloe's meal plan
for the week was on the wall.

Mexico Monday

Sushi Tuesday

Wednoodlesday

Thai-ursday

Friedchickensday

'OK, Docter Noel,' I said to myself. 'It's Sushi Tuesday, so let's just make some sushi! Wait . . . How do you make sushi?'

Looking in Gretel's Japanese cookbook, I was struck by

HOW MANY DANGEROUS INGREDIENTS THERE ARE IN SUSHI.

Seaweed? Well, that could have crabs or lobsters living in it.

Carrots? **MUCH** too pointy.

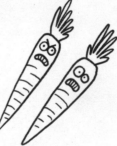

Raw fish? **RAW FISH?** What if the fish is still alive?
AND WHAT IF THAT FISH IS A SHARK?

No, no, no, no x 1,000,000

I decided to try something a little safer for my first
  day. Looking around the kitchen, my eyes were
  immediately drawn to a big basket in the corner.

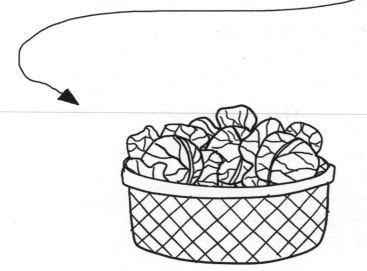

'A-HA!'

I picked up the chalk and made a small alteration
  to today's meal plan.

~~Sushi Tuesday~~
CABBAGE SOUP TUESDAY

And then I had an idea. If I could use up all of these cabbages today, and think of a recipe that also used cabbages for tomorrow, then I could call in on Gretel tonight to order more cabbages.

Then I had an **EVEN** better idea . . . and changed the meal plan for the week: ⟶

~~Mexico Monday~~

Cabbage Soup Tuesday

~~Sushi Tuesday~~

wedCABBAGESOUPday

~~Wednoodlesday~~

CABBAGE SOUP THURSDAY

~~Thai-ursday~~

SURPRISE DAY FRIDAY!

~~Friedchickensday~~

SURPRISE = more CABBAGE SOUP!!!

Just then, Teddy burst into the kitchen. He had tears running down his cheeks.

'Oh no! What's wrong?'

'Uncle N-N-Noel, you know
I cycle in to school on Liam every morning
with my sisters?'

'Yes I do,' I said, shaking my head disapprovingly.

'Well, I just went out to say hello to him and
he's . . .' Teddy could barely speak.

'Go on, Teddy,' I said.

'He's g-g-gone! **WAAH-WEE! WAAH-WEE!**' Teddy almost
never cried, but when he did he made a sound like
a backwards ambulance.

'This has gone too far!' I said. 'Come on, we're going to see Mr Staples.'

NOTE: Even though bicycles are **RAD** (**R**eally **A**wfully **D**angerous), one of the **MOST IMPORTANT** rules of Level 3 **DANGEROLOGY** is to help a fellow **DANGEROLOGIST** when things go wrong.

Mr Staples phoned the police station and soon Jane the policewoman arrived to examine the latest crime scene.

'Oh, it's you,' she said when she saw me. 'I hope you haven't done anything dangerous here yet — like knocking over a bookshelf or getting anybody stuck in a basketball hoop.'

'Absolutely not!' I said. 'I'm actually very safe.'

'This is juuust awful,' said Mr Staples, who was nearly as sad as Teddy. 'How can this be happening in my schoool?'

'Do you have any idea who is doing it?' I asked Jane. 'Do you have any leads?'

NOTE: I am not a detective, but I wanted to let her know that I can speak the lingo.

'Not at the moment.' And then she came in close to my ear. 'Can you look out for anything suspicious? I'm pretty sure it's someone at the school, maybe a group.'

'Leave it with me,' I said.

It was strange to suddenly care about my least favourite objects in the world, but I could see how much Liam meant to Teddy. Also, I really wanted to show Jane that **I AM NOT DANGEROUS.**

As Teddy and I left Staples' office, we passed the BMX gang, who were hanging around outside the sports hall, waiting for PE.

'Well, well, well, if it isn't Captain Cape himself,' said Sunglasses.

'Are you here to teach us Helmetology?' asked Hood.

'No, I am not,' I said. 'I'm here to cook. But also to get to the bottom of this bicycle mystery. I don't suppose you know anything?'

'Oh, so you fight crime too! What's your superhero name? Beardman?' said Sunglasses.

'Captain Bum Bag?' said Hood.

'What will you do if you find who's taking the bikes? Crash into the thief in your shopping trolley?' said Hat.

'Fire them into a hedge?' added Sunglasses.

'Contact the police?' asked Spike.

They all turned to stare at him.

'Excuse me,' I said. 'I have a very large meal to prepare. Come on, Teddy.'

I spent the morning chopping cabbages and loading them into a pot big enough to swim in.

NOTE: Never swim in soup. In fact, never swim.

NOTE 2: From a **DANGEROLOGY** perspective, it's best not to heat soup **TOO HOT.**

NOTE 3: I also find eating slightly cold cabbage soup brings out the **DELICIOUS CABBAGEY FLAVOURS.**

How did my first meal go?

Well, let's just say that I was **VERY** pleased and, although initially surprised, all the students and teachers who filled the long tables in the cafeteria ate in **COMPLETE SILENCE.** And they found the soup so filling that **NOBODY ASKED FOR MORE** or wanted a scoop of the delicious cabbage ice cream I had prepared for dessert.

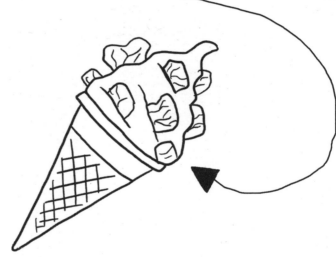

JOB DONE!

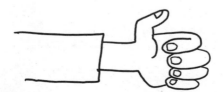

TUESDAY AFTERNOON — A SCARY BREAKTHROUGH

I was clearing up the bowls after lunch when
Teddy rushed back into the kitchen. 'Liam has
come b-b-back!'

'Well, that's great news! Maybe someone just
borrowed him!'

But Teddy didn't seem very happy. He was shaking
his head, and he pulled me out to where the bicycles
were parked.

I tried to be as upbeat as possible about what we
could see. 'Well, a **LOT** of your bike has
come back, Teddy. The main bit is certainly there.
And look — the pedals . . . Or, one of them . . .'

Who would do this? And why?

'I'll get to the bottom of this mystery, I promise. We just need a clue . . . **LOOK!**'

Parked at the end of the line of bicycles was something else.

THE MOST DANGEROUS WHIZZY VEHICLE OF ALL:

A SEGWAY.

And, to a Level 5 **DANGEROLOGIST** such as myself, a Segway is a sign of only one thing.

VAMPIRES.

'Teddy, I believe there may be vampires operating in this school. And, if they're here, they are sure to be behind these thefts.'

'R-r-really?' said Teddy.

I nodded my head. 'Tomorrow morning, we go vampire hunting.'

This evening I called in to Gretel's to order more cabbages. As I may have said before, Gretel is the most beautiful and intelligent person in the world, and however beautiful and intelligent you are imagining her to be, she is even more beautiful and intelligent than that.

For a long time, I was too scared to speak to her, but now I call in whenever I have something

VERY IMPORTANT to talk to her about.

In the last week **VERY IMPORTANT THINGS** have included:

- 'Do you think it'll rain tomorrow?'

- 'I saw a bee in your garden.'

- 'What date is your birthday?'

- 'What date is your birthday again?' (I'd forgotten as I was worried about the bee.)

- Delivering the special **DANGER HELMET** I had made for her birthday.

- Thanking her for the card she had posted to **THE DANGERZONE** to thank me for the **DANGER HELMET.**

- 'Can I borrow all your cookbooks?'

NOELTY-ONE

'They must really love cabbages,' she said when I asked her to deliver fifty of them.

'Oh, Gretel, everyone loves **YOUR** cabbages!'

I was about to tell her about the bicycles and the vampires, when someone called my name.

'NOEL!'

I turned round, but couldn't see anyone.

Then: **'NOEL, NOEL.'**

'You'll have to excuse me, Gretel. It sounds like somebody needs me!'

I ran out to the street, and this time the voice said,

'COME HERE, NOEL!'

It seemed to be coming from the direction of my house.

Was somebody **TRAPPED IN THE DANGERZONE?**

Then I heard it again.

'NOEL! PLEASE!'

IT WAS COMING FROM THE DANGERGARDEN! Maybe
my other neighbours, David and Chris, were in trouble?
Had there been an accident? Maybe the bee had

returned! Or could it be **AN ALLEAFGATOR?**

NOELTY-THREE

I burst out of the back door. 'NOBODY PANIC!
DOCTER NOEL ZONE IS HERE.'

And then I heard all the zookeepers laugh.

'Sorry!' Roxanne the head zookeeper called over
the wall. 'We were trying to get Noel the giraffe
to come over for his dinner.'

To make matters worse, as soon as Noel the giraffe
saw me, he started doing his annoying
happy-giraffe-smiling-and-dancing thing, while they
all laughed again.

'You ruined my conversation with Gretel for this?'
I whispered in his direction, before turning round
and going straight to bed, in my bath.

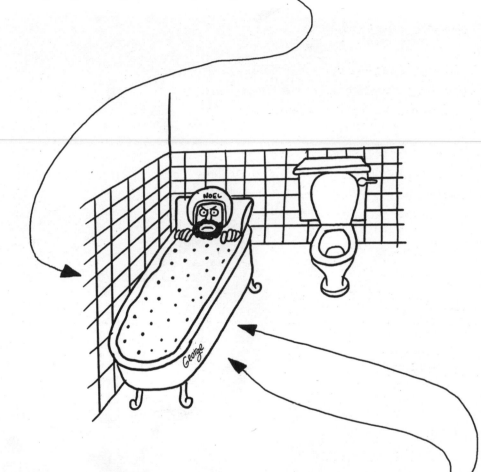

NOTE: I sleep in the bath. It is the safest place to sleep.

NOTE 2: I call my bath **GEORGE.**

NOELTY-FIVE

It was still dark when Teddy and I arrived at the main door of the school this morning.

'L -L-Look!' Teddy whispered. Two more half bikes were parked in the racks.

'So the thief has struck again!' I said. 'Soon we're going to break this case wide open and this thief will be doing a long stretch in the clink.'

'What does that mean?' asked Teddy.

'I'm not sure exactly. It's what detectives say.'

As I pushed the door open, it burped a long, slow creak down the dark corridor.

'W-w-what are we l-l-looking for, Uncle N-N-Noel?' Teddy whispered.

'Any classic signs of vampire activity, nephew. Teachers asleep upside down, bats, any indication of paper-eating — vampires **LOVE** to eat paper. And of course we need to listen out for loud vampire laughs or farts. Can you remember how vampire farts sound?'

'Oh, I know this!' said Teddy. 'Is it **PAAAARP**?'

'Close. That's actually the dreaded parp donkey, the stinkiest farter in the animal kingdom. Vampire farts go **HOOOONNNNK**.'

'Got it!' said Teddy. My **DASK** was learning fast.

'Right, helmet lights **ON**,' I whispered.

NOELTY-SEVEN

Our beams lit two small puddles of light in front of us that bounced shadows on to the hundreds of tiny faces in the photos that filled the walls.

'I'm s-s-scared,' said Teddy.

'There's nothing to be afraid of, Teddy. You are with the greatest **DANGEROLOGIST** in the woAAAAAGH!'

'A black shadow was moving down the corridor
towards us — a black shadow that made a strange
  trundling sound.

'It's some kind of half monster, half machine!' I cried.

'Oh, that's Spangles,' said Teddy.

'Who?'

'Spangles. She's the school cat. She had an accident
a few years ago, so they gave her wheels,' Teddy
  explained.

NOTE: I don't usually like cats (**THEY COULD BE TIGERS**), and you know how I feel about whizzy things. But it was impossible not to like Spangles. Also, she had reversed between our **DANGERBOOTS** and looked like she really wanted to help.

'OK, Spangles,' I whispered. 'You can join the vampire hunt.'

Every step seemed to creak as Teddy, Spangles and I slowly made our way down the corridor, checking in every room or cupboard where vampires might lurk. As we peered into one classroom, my helmet light picked out a bony hand . . .

then moved up to a bony arm . . .

then to two hollow spaces in a skull where eyes should be!

I dropped to my knees. 'AAAAGH, it's Springy Staples!
The vampires have got to him. Oh, Springy, we're
too late, I'm sorry . . .'

Then Teddy pointed out that this was the science room,
and it was a plastic skeleton.

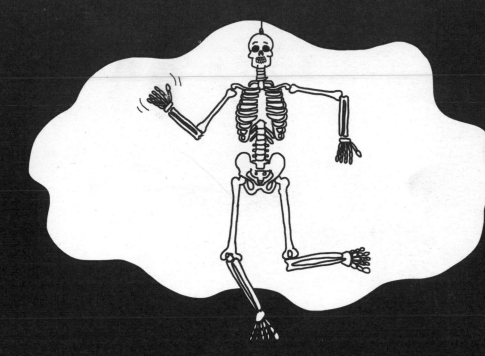

'As I suspected,' I said. 'I was just testing you, Teddy.
All part of your **DANGEROLOGY** training.' And we
carried on.

At the very end of the ground-floor corridor was a
cupboard with a much bigger door than the rest.
It had a combination padlock dangling from the handle.

'**VERY** suspicious,' I said. 'This is the only locked door
we've come across. We'll have to check inside.
  I have a real knack for opening these, Teddy.
  You see, it's always three numbers that are obvious.
Try one-one-one.'

Teddy set the lock to these numbers, but it didn't open.

'OK, no problem: try two-two-two.'

Teddy tried these and it still didn't work.

  'Go with one-two-three.'

'That's not it, Uncle.'

  'Then three-two-one.'

'Still no,' said Teddy.

'Wait, we have to think . . . What number would vampires choose? I've got it! Zero-zero-zero, because that looks like **OOO**, which is a scary sound like **WOOO**.'

'Doesn't work, Uncle.'

'We are so close. Let's just try a couple more!'

Twenty minutes later, we were still trying. We had
put in the start of the school's phone number, the
end of the school's phone number, the street number
of the school, Springy's car registration,

NOEL-NOEL-NOEL, NOEL-eight-seven, but nothing.

'Uncle, it'll be g-g-getting light s-s-soon and
everyone will be coming in to school.'

'Good point,' I said. 'Make a note of this cupboard in

your **PORB** and we'll come back and open it
another time.'

'This is corridor number two and this is the . . . ten,
eleven, t-t-twelfth door . . .' Teddy said as he noted
down the location of the cupboard.

'**UNCLE!** Maybe that's the number! Two-one-two!'

'No,' I said, shaking my head. 'It's always an obvious number, but that's much too obvious —'

'IT WORKS!' whispered Teddy. The lock had popped open in his hand.

'Great work, Teddy!' I said.

The door opened a few inches and immediately Spangles dashed inside.

'No, Spangles!' I said. 'You'll get chomped!'

When we shone our lights inside, I couldn't believe what we had found. 'This must be the vampires' kitchen, Teddy! Look at all the paper!'

'From this amount, I would estimate there must be at least one hundred vampires operating in this school,' I said.

'Erm, U-U-Uncle.'

'What is it?' I said.

Teddy was pointing at a sign on the wall. 'I don't think this is the vampires' kitchen.'

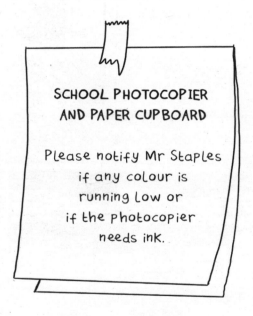

SCHOOL PHOTOCOPIER
AND PAPER CUPBOARD

Please notify Mr Staples
if any colour is
running low or
if the photocopier
needs ink.

'Ah, I see. Forget what I just said.'

'Uncle, m-m-maybe there aren't any v-v-vam—'

HOOOOOOOONNNNK!

That dreadful sound filled the air and, for a moment, we froze.

'V-v-vampire f-f-fart!' Teddy mouthed at me.

It came from behind the door directly across the corridor. Teddy moved behind me and gripped my leg.

'No, Teddy! Don't panic!

we are **DANGEROLOGISTS.**

WE NEVER PANIC!'

I advanced towards the door with Teddy clamped round my **DANGERBOOT.**

Then it happened again.

HOOOOOOOONNNNK!

We both sprinted back into the paper cupboard.

'OK, this is getting serious. Remove your baguette,'
I said.

NOTE: Vampires, as I'm sure you know, **HATE** garlic.
They can't even be in the same room as it.
  So that morning I had taken two emergency
garlic breads out of my freezer and put them
into our **PEBB**s.

  'But it's still so c-c-cold,' said Teddy, lifting his out.

'That bread could save your life.'

My plan was to hide in the cupboard till whatever was in there came out. But Spangles isn't a Level 5

DANGEROLOGIST and she had another idea.

She trundled up to the door, pushed her paw against it and slowly began to edge her wheels forward.

'NO! SPANGLES!' I ran to pick her up, but, as I bent over, the door to the classroom swung open.

I held up my garlic bread and prepared for the worst.

HUNDRED AND NOEL

'Who's there?' bellowed a voice like a goat singing an opera. Its owner, a lady with her hair piled up on her head like an ice-cream cone, was sitting at a huge organ. Pipes, tubes and intricate mechanical parts filled the wall behind her.

'How dare you interrupt me while I'm working on my keyboard!' She banged down on the keys and

another deafening **HOOOOOOOONNNNK** filled the school.

'I'm so sorry. I was just passing and . . . . it's very loud,' I said.

'So what if it is?' she said, angrily pulling across a big wooden shutter in front of the organ. 'Soon it's going

to be the **LOUDEST ORGAN IN THE WORLD** and

EVERYONE WILL HEAR MY MUSIC!' She shouted the last part in case I didn't understand what the word 'loud' meant. 'Who are you?'

'I'm the new chef.'

'Why are you waving a baguette at me?'

There was no way I could tell her the real reason,
  so I just said the first thing that came into my head.

'We're doing taste tests for my new bread. I was
  just wondering if you'd like to try it?'

'It's frozen, you moron.' And then she came in really close to my face. 'I like bread, but I'll tell you what I don't like: snoopy people snooping around here, dressed like they've just been fired from a circus cannon.' And with that she slammed the door of the music room in my face.

'She's definitely not a vampire,' I said to Teddy, as we walked back towards the kitchen. 'She didn't react to the garlic.'

'That's Mrs Waddock. She's the g-g-grumpiest teacher in the whole school,' said Teddy.

The sun was coming up and the empty corridors
would soon be bustling with students. But for now they
were still eerily quiet. Suddenly Teddy jumped.

'U–U–Uncle Noel! IS T–T–THAT A W–W–WITCH?'

'Teddy! That's not a very nice way to speak about
Mrs Waddock. Maybe she's just having a bad day.'

'N–N–NO! OVER T–T–THERE!' A hideous shape in a
pointy hat was floating past the big window beside
us. It stopped with an awful screeeeeeeech at the
door just up ahead.

Teddy and I dived on to the floor in terror.

The door creeeeaaaaked open and standing there, with a large basket of cabbages on the front of her bike, was Gretel.

'Hi, Noel! Are you OK down there?'

'Oh yes, absolutely, Gretel! I was just showing my nephew Teddy here how to check if, erm, there's a volcano underneath your school. We were listening for rumbles. It could unexpectedly knock you over.'

'Well, I'll be safe with this!' she said, pointing at her **DANGER HELMET.**
She made it look more beautiful than I thought any

DANGER HELMET
could ever look.

NOTE: And that is **VERY** beautiful.

'I'd better drop these cabbages off and continue with my deliveries. What are you going to make today?'

'Classic cabbage soup again today, Gretel. This time with a twist.'

'A twist? I hope they all like it!'

As she cycled off, I thought, 'I wish she didn't cycle. But, when she does, she cycles more beautifully than anyone else.'

As Gretel went out through the school gates, Mr Staples was just coming in.

ON

HIS

SEGWAY.

'Very interesting,' I said, making a note in my **PORB.** 'Very interesting indeed.'

'We didn't find any v-v-vampires, Uncle. Does that m-m-mean there aren't any in the school?'

'There still could be a vampire, Teddy,' I said. 'And, if there is, we will find him at lunch today. I have another plan!'

'What do vampires really hate?' I asked Teddy as he stirred the new batch of cabbage soup.

'T–T–Tickling?'

'No, that's werewolves.'

'Rain?'

'No, that's robots. They go rusty.'

'B–b–blowing b–b–bubbles?'

'No, that's ghosts. Remember this morning? Come on, Teddy!'

He had run out of ideas, so I tried to give him a clue. 'Begins with a G? Gar . . . Gar . . .'

'G–G–Gardening?'

'No, gar**LIC!**' I said. 'Now pass me that big bucket.'

'What's in it? Pew, it really stinks.'

'Garlic. A lot of garlic. And so it's

not **TOO** obvious I've mixed it up
with a jar of spices I found in
the cupboard.'

Teddy and I watched the whole school file in for lunch.
From the groans that went round the cafeteria, nobody
seemed overly excited to be receiving cabbage soup
again. But they were hungry and soon tucked in.

'Now let's wait and see who runs out of the cafeteria
first,' I said as we looked on from the serving hatch.

'Get ready with your **PORB**, Teddy.'

It only took a few moments before the first
shot up from their seat.

'SPRINGY!' said Teddy.

The headmaster stood up and started to shake his
head from side to side.

HUNDRED AND NOELTEEN

'Well this, you would haaave to say, is a raaather flavoursome soup —' he stuck his tongue out —

'to a very great extent ATISHOO . . .'

And he began to sneeze very loud, yelling sneezes.

AATISHOO

ATISHOO

AAATISHOO

AATISHOO

'WHOA!' said Teddy.

'I knew it! That's how he's always popping up,' I said.

'BECAUSE HE CAN TURN INTO A BAT!'

'And he's still b-b-boring,' Teddy said. 'He must be the m-m-most b-b-boring vampire ever.'

Then Mrs Waddock stood up and started to do the same thing. '**ATISHOO! ATISHOO!** This tastes like a bin full of sick!'

'So the organ was just to throw us off her vampire fart scent! She and Staples are in this together!' I cried.

Then the whole BMX gang stood up. They all had their tongues out and were jumping up and down, sneezing.

Teddy couldn't believe it. 'There are **S-S-SO** many vampires in this s-s-school!'

But then Teddy's sisters, Katherine and Millicent, stood up. And so did every single person sitting at their table.

'What's going on?' I said.

'**WAAA!**' Teddy had taken a few spoonfuls of his soup and now **HE** was now jumping up and down, waving his hands around.

'I p-p-promise I'm not a **ATISHOO–ATISHOO** a vampire, Uncle Noel, I p-p-prom-**ATISHOO!** I think there's just . . . just . . . a bit t-t-too much s-s-spice in the **ATISH**oup.'

By this point, every single person in the cafeteria was on their feet, sneezing and jumping around. But no one had left the room. Now we could be sure: there were no vampires in the school.

Mr Staples made his way to the serving hatch.

'Doctor Zooone-**ATISHOO**. I thiiiink it might **ATISHOO** be sensible to give you a break from your **ATISHOO** cooking duuuties and mooove you to another section of the **ATISHOO** school for the rest of the weeek.'

I thought about it for a moment. Sure, I'd miss the kitchen, but now I could search for clues in other parts of the school. I only had a few days left before Chloe came back, and I had promised Teddy I'd find the rest of Liam.

While I've got some time before my next job, let me take a moment to point out another **INCREDIBLY SNEAKY SCHOOL BEAST** that every LEVEL 3 Dangerologist should be aware of.

AAAAaAAA

(Advice About Avoiding Angry and Aggressive Animal Attacks)

The Classroom Chameleon

DANGEROLOGISTS should **ALWAYS** be on the lookout for dangerous animals. But with this one you'll need to look really, **REALLY** closely. That's because **THE CLASSROOM CHAMELEON**, like other members of the chameleon lizard family, has the ability to blend perfectly into its background.

There is one hiding on this globe.

CLUE: It's where you find **KANGAROOS.**

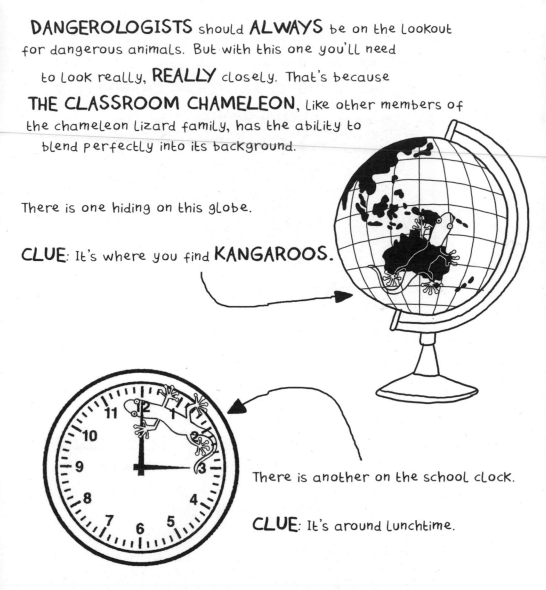

There is another on the school clock.

CLUE: It's around lunchtime.

Now, you probably think that this sounds great.
Oh, it'd be such fun to have a lizard living in your
school, scampering up walls, occasionally giving
your schoolmates a fright.

But you will change your mind when I tell you
what it eats. You see, **THE CLASSROOM CHAMELEON**
lives entirely on a diet of **HOMEWORK.** It burrows
into school bags to find the **FRESHEST HOMEWORK** it can.
And then

CHOMP!

CHOMP!

CHOMP!

The worst part is, because they are **SO WELL DISGUISED,**
teachers never see them and refuse to believe they exist.

So when you say, 'A lizard ate my homework,'
they will think you have made up a terrible
excuse, and you will be in **BIG** trouble.

HOW TO KEEP THE CLASSROOM CHAMELEON AWAY

It's very simple. Like many animals (and I include students in this), **THE CLASSROOM CHAMELEON HATES MATHS.** Just leave some long division or multiplication on your desk or on top of your school bag and this will be enough to scare it away.

As the **GREATEST DANGEROLOGIST IN THE WORLD,
EVER** (thank you), I know **ALL** about **DANGER.**

I have lifted toilet seats in bathrooms where
THERE COULD BE A TOILET SHARK.

I have checked to see if bus stops
are really **BUS-STOP COBRAS.**

BUS

**I HAVE *LOOKED* AFTER MY SISTER'S
DOG, NAPKIN, FOR AN ENTIRE WEEK.**

But none of these things prepared me for the new job that Mr Staples gave me . . .

I have now been exposed to a level of **DANGER** worse than **RAD** (**R**eally **A**wfully **D**angerous — the highest level of **DANGER** I had previously thought possible). I spent this afternoon at

That name would make you think that they are
going to grow up to be cute fluffy sheep. But these
little monsters aren't going to grow up to be sheep.

THEY ARE GOING TO GROW UP TO BE BIG MONSTERS.

I began by trying to explain the simplest basics of **DANGEROLOGY**, but they just wanted to dive into the ball pool and hang off my **T-COD.** Then, when I asked if they had any questions, what did they say to me?

So I decided to create this beautiful and informative poster, which can hang on their wall, and I hope they will learn from it in the future.

ABC of DANGER

A is for **ALLEAFGATOR**
under an **APPLE TREE**

B is for **BEAR ON**
A BOUNCY CASTLE

C is for **CABBALANCHE**
(Cabbage Avalanche)

D is for
DINOSAUR DENTIST

E is for **ELEPHANTOM**

F is for **FLIP-FLOPS**
on **FIRE**

G is for **GIDDY GIRAFFE**

H is for **HEDGEHOG**
in your **HELMET**

I is for **ICY ICE**

J is for
JET-SKI JOUSTING

K is for **KANGAROO**
with a **KITE**

L is for **LOBSTER**
in your **LOO**

M is for
MATADOR MUMMY

N is for **NO CABBAGES**
(Not dangerous, just bad)

O is for
OCTOPUSHCHAIR

P is for **PARP**
DONKEY PARTY

Q is for **QUEUE OF**
QUEEN BEES

R is **ROBOT RHINOCEROS**

S is for **STINGRAY SUSHI**

T is for
TERRIFYING TREE

U is for
UNKIND UNDERPANTS

V is for
VAMPIRE VOLCANO

W is for
WEREWOLF WASP

X is for **XEME**
POOPING ON A XERUS *

Y is for **YELLING YETI**

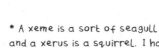

Z is for
ZOMBIE ZEBRA

* A xeme is a sort of seagull
and a xerus is a squirrel. I had
to look these up in the dictionary.

I must have been concentrating too hard on my artwork, because when I turned round, the room was empty.

I checked in the ball pool, under the mountain of soft toys and behind the coats. Then I noticed the back door of *Little Lambs* was wide open and the childproof gate had been kicked over.

THEY HAD ALL ESCAPED.

I don't know much about being a nursery-school teacher, but I'm pretty sure the number one rule is:

MAKE SURE YOU DON'T LOSE ALL OF THE CHILDREN.

This was a **DANGEMERGENCY,** and **DANGEMERGENCIES** require **DRASTIC ACTION.** And sometimes **DRASTIC ACTION** involves whizzy vehicles.

I ran outside to where Mr Staples' Segway was parked, jumped on it and set off around the school grounds, in search of the lost Lambs.

I found the first one wandering round the running track, which was being mowed, ready for Saturday's sports day.

I found another on her way up a tree in the wooded area beside the track.

The next one was hidden in the cabbage basket in the Kitchen, and another was lying beside Spangles in her cat bed.

There were still two more to go.

One had managed to get into the paper cupboard
and was inside a large envelope — maybe
  the combination lock on the door was easier to open
    than I thought.

There was still one left. I went back outside to where the bicycles were parked and found the BMX gang standing there suspiciously.

'Why aren't you in class?' I asked. 'Not thinking about stealing any bikes, I hope.'

'No way, Doctor Dre,' said Sunglasses. 'We're guarding them, making sure the thief doesn't strike again.'

I wasn't sure whether to believe her, but I had another, more pressing issue on my mind.

'Did any of you see a small child around here?'

'Haven't seen a thing,' said Hood. 'Oh, apart from that one who climbed into Mrs Waddock's car a few minutes ago.'

'Which car is that?' I demanded.

'THE ONE COMING TOWARDS US!' they all screamed.

A green car was rolling directly towards us. At the wheel, the last *Little Lamb* was laughing hysterically to himself as he had just figured out how to release a handbrake.

The BMX gang scattered as I sprinted towards the car and, with five toddlers still clinging to me, jumped in the passenger door.

I pulled up the handbrake just as we were about to crash into the main door of the school.

Even the *Little Lambs* were impressed. They gave me a round of applause.

'Hey, what do you think you're doing?' bleated an awful voice from an upstairs window. It was Mrs Waddock. 'I've caught you red-handed, stealing my car. I suppose you've been robbing the bikes too!'

'I have not!' I said. 'I would never . . .' But the window had slammed shut.

'WHAAAT ON EARTH IS GOING ON?' said Mr Staples, springing out from nowhere.

I tried to explain about the escape and how this had all come about, but Springy wasn't listening.
He seemed distracted. There was a note of panic in his still-boring voice.

'In thiiirty years at this school, this has beeen my most difficult week. I'm going to give you a new job tomorrow, Doctor Zone, but can you please make sure that nothing else unexpected happens?'

Poor Springy Staples. He was so stressed.

'Yes, of course!' I said. Now, more than ever, he needed me to catch this thief.

This evening Teddy came over and we both tried to sketch Liam to remind us how he looked when he had all of his parts.

Teddy managed not to cry, but I could tell it was difficult for him. 'He had a ding-dingy bell, and a water bottle that made ordinary water taste like, like . . . magic water.'

Our pictures were quite different, but both captured important sides of Liam's personality.

'What happened to your **PEBB**?' Teddy asked, pointing at a big hole in the side of it.

It had been chomped by a Little Lamb.

'Maybe one of them is secretly a bag-eating robot and is going around the school eating everything that is made of bag,' he said.

Teddy was only five, so he often said ridiculous things like . . .

'**WAIT** . . . That's **IT**! Teddy, that **MUST** be what is going on with the bikes! It's so obvious now! There must be **A ROBOT** in the school that is snacking on them! And tomorrow we are going to find it!'

When I called in to Mr Staples' office this morning, he was weeping into his wastepaper basket. Three more bicycles had disappeared during the night and his Segway had gone too.

'I'm sure we haven't seen the last of it,' I said.
'Well, some of it, anyway.'

He looked like he hadn't slept.

'If awful things keep happening,' he mumbled, 'maybe I shouldn't be the headmaster of this school any more.'

The sad **HOOOOOOOONNNNN**
rang out across the school. It seemed t̶
for how Mr Staples was feeling.

'Don't say that,' I said. 'You are the boss! You are
Mr Staples! You hold this whole school together, like
a . . . a staple. And sometimes staples have a tough
week, getting pulled and bent around. But they never
break. Except for some of them. But you are not one of
those ones.'

It wasn't my best speech, but it seemed to do the trick.
'You're right, Doctor! You're absolutely right. I have
to keep going. I mean, I bet that was just a run of
rotten luck.'

'Yeah!' I said.

...of Mrs Waddock's organ ...the right music

...charge of the final ...play, before the world ...on. The entire school will be

This was ...t news.
If everyone ...as going to
be there, then I'd be in the
same room as the robot.
This would be my chance
to catch it, and I knew
exactly how.

The school play was called 'The Warrior Princess and the Silver Sword' and the cast included my nieces,

Katherine and Millicent. They were **NOT** delighted to see me take charge and, as I watched them rehearse,

I was **NOT** delighted with their play either.

But I know that actors and actresses can be very sensitive, so, before saying what I didn't like about it, I pointed out a few things I did like.

'I like your costume, Katherine — dressed in your suit
of armour as the Warrior Princess. Very safe!
And I like that horse,' I said, pointing at Hood and
   Millicent, who were inside the horse costume.
'Much safer than a real horse. But I don't like
   anything else, so we have to change it all for the
opening this afternoon, OK? Let's go to work!'

If I had to narrow it down, my main problem with
the play was the entire story. 'The Warrior Princess
   and the Silver Sword' was the tale of a shy princess
who one day finds a sword in a river, which she uses
   to slay all of the dragons that have been terrorizing
   her village.

'I have a couple of small alterations,' I began. 'We are going to change "dragons" to "friends". And instead of slaying them, we'll have the princess make a delicious meal for them. Oh, and instead of finding a sword, she finds some cabbages.'

'This is ridiculous,' said Millicent. 'I mean, how would she find cabbages in a river?'

'That's a good point,' I said. 'We'll get rid of the river too and replace it with a field. She grows them.'

'So you are changing our story from dragon-slaying to making cabbage dinner for friends?' said Katherine.

'Yes, you've got it!
    That's the new title:
    "Making Cabbage Dinner for Friends".'

After lunch, the whole school packed into the assembly hall for the first and, unfortunately, only ever performance of 'Making Cabbage Dinner for Friends'.

I had worked out an ingenious plan to find the robo-thief, and, as the play started, it began to take effect.

When Warrior Princess Katherine came out in her suit of armour, she floated up into the air.

'Whoa!' said Teddy, who was sitting beside me.

'The special e-e-effects in this play are **INCREDIBLE.**'

The floaty effect was caused by the enormous magnet I had
borrowed from my friend Cornelius at the scrapyard
  and had lowered over the roof of the assembly hall.

The problem with a magnet, however, is that it doesn't choose
  what to lift, and soon everything that had metal in
it was rising upwards. First it was the pen in
  Mr Staples' shirt pocket, then the teachers' keys
  and mobile phones, then Spangles and her wheels.

After a while, our chairs started to shake — gently at first, before suddenly throwing us all on to the floor as they shot up to the ceiling. They narrowly missed Katherine and Spangles, who were both looking

VERY confused and unhappy.

'STOP THE PLAAAY!' screamed Springy Staples, who was now more agitated than I'd ever seen him before. 'What on earth is goooing on? Can aaanyone please explain what is happening?'

There was silence for a moment, then I stood up and raised my hand. 'It's my fault,' I said. 'I thought a robot might have been eating the bikes, so I tried to find it with a big magnet.'

'**YOOOOU THOUGHT WHAAAT?**' Springy's face had gone
bright red and his normally perfect hair was a mess.
He was jabbing a bony finger in my direction.

'Zone, your arriiival at this schoool has resulted in the mooost
bizarre events I have witnessed in all my time as a teacher.
A mass soup-poisoning in the cafeteria? An infant driving a car
in to school? And now you've maaanaged to get a student and a
cat stuck to the ceeeiling!'

'Sorry,' I said, looking down at the floor.

But Mr Staples wasn't finished. 'You are a **DAAANGER**
to this school. Go out of that door **NOW** and neeever,
eeever cooome baaack.'

The squeak of my footwear was the only sound in the hall as I made my way to the exit. When I reached the door, I turned round.

'I'm sorry my **DANGERBOOTS** are loud. And I'm sorry these last few days haven't worked out as well as I'd hoped. But I was just trying really hard to find your bikes. That's supposed to be the motto of this school, isn't it? "Please Try Really Hard"? Goodbye.'

'Come back!' said one voice.

'Really? You want me to stay?'

'No, I'm still stuck up here.' It was Katherine.

'Oh, I'll get a ladder,' I said.

'NO!' yelled Springy. **'YOU JUST GO.'**

I trudged off, out of the gate and home to **THE DANGERZONE.**

I barely slept last night, tossing and turning in George. The voices of Jane the policewoman, Mrs Waddock and Mr Staples were echoing round my head.

It made one thing clear: I have to catch whoever is stealing these bikes.

It's the only way I can show **EVERYONE** who **DOCTER NOEL ZONE** really is.

In my **PORB** I had narrowed down the list of suspects. Now there was only one left:

LIST OF SUSPECTS
~~Vampires~~
~~Mr Staples~~
~~Robots~~
The BMX gang

But I would need to catch them **IN THE ACT** of stealing a bicycle. And this would require a trip to the . . .

WOD

(Wardrobe Of Disguise)

Being **THE GREATEST DANGEROLGIST IN THE WORLD** has advantages and disadvantages. The main advantage is that people act **MORE SAFELY** when you are around. They see you coming and tie their shoelaces and keep their dog on its lead. The main disadvantage is that, because everyone is doing their best to act safely, sometimes it is hard for you to see where the **DANGER** really is.

It is for this reason that, hidden inside an old fridge in my kitchen, I keep my **WOD.**

FRIDGE

NOTE: My Wardrobe Of Disguise is in disguise itself.

HUNDRED AND FIFTY-NOEL

This allows me to travel around 100% unNOELticed.

(UNNOTICED + ME = UNNOELTICED)

Some of my **BEST DISGUISES** include:

1.
Ms Noelle Zone, the nosy parking warden

2.
Old Noel, the friendly retired sea captain

3.
Cocker SpaNoel, the cute big-eared dog that keeps an eye on things

4.
Noel the Lamp Post — he can see in the dark.

But this wasn't a job for any of them. I needed a
special disguise — something that you'd find in a school.

In the back of the **WOD** I found the perfect thing:

DOCTER BIN — he's not afraid to get his hands dirty.

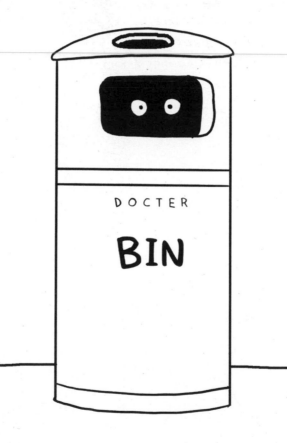

I got to school before anyone else this morning.

NOTE: The journey took a long time because you're not allowed to move very fast when you're a bin.

I took up a position close to the bicycle racks, where I observed that two more half bikes had come back during the night.

DOCTER

BIN

Soon the last few people who still had bicycles arrived and locked them to the racks. Everyone seemed to be talking about tomorrow's sports day. Teddy arrived and checked to see if the rest of Liam had reappeared. It hadn't and he looked so sad. I felt like telling him I would find it, but then remembered I was a bin.

At one point I nearly dozed off, but was I woken by another of Mrs Waddock's **HOOOOOOOONNNNK**s.

Then came morning break. I should really have been expecting it, but at least a hundred students finished their drinks and snacks and shoved them into my slot. Teachers poured half cups of cold coffee into me and Spangles did what cats do against me. Well, I couldn't just get out and walk away. Especially as I was banned from the school.

But soon the BMX gang were standing round me, practising their incredibly dangerous BMX tricks.

I couldn't hear what they were saying till Hat turned and looked in my direction. 'That bin is new. Let's try to jump over it!'

I held my breath.

'It's too high, said Sunglasses, as they circled me. But my relief didn't last long. 'Let's roll it down the hill!'

DOCTER

BIN

To my horror, they carried me to the back of the sports field and then rolled me down the hill eight or

NOEL times, whooping with delight whenever they managed to make me go further than the last roll.

I was very glad to hear the bell ringing in the distance for the end of lunch.

'What'll we do with this?' said Hood.

'Throw it in the river! See if it floats,' said Hat.

'No. Springy will be furious,' said Sunglasses. 'He might throw us out of the school like he did with Crash-helmet Clarence yesterday!'

I quite liked that name, to be honest.

They rolled me back and tried to find the exact spot where I had been.

'Was it here?' asked Sunglasses.

'No, here,' replied Hood.

DOCTER
BIN

Much to my annoyance, I was facing the wrong
  direction and couldn't see what happened next.

  'No, I'm pretty sure it was . . .'

Slowly Hat's voice trailed off and Spike started to
  whimper.

'UH–UH–UH–UH–UH! NO_{ooo}OOOO_{ooo}O!'

**'AAAAAAAAGH, OUR BIKES!
THEY'RE ALL GONE! AAAAAAAAGH.'**

Despite what they had just done to me, it was
impossible not to feel sorry for them. Now they were
the No-BMX Gang.

But it also meant that I had **NO** suspects left on my list.

It was time for my

EMERGENCY
LAST RESORT
DANGERPLAN.

FRIDAY, MIDNIGHT — TEDDY IN THE MIDDLE

'I d-d-don't understand why you n-n-need me,'
whispered my nephew as I helped him over the wall
beside the locked school gates. It was really dark.
Every light in the school was off and this time we
weren't using our helmet lamps.

'I need you because every mousetrap needs a piece
of cheese, Teddy. And when the mouse tries to take the
cheese I'll be able to see who the mouse is.'

'I w-w-wish you were the ch-ch-cheese,' said Teddy.

'No. I'm more like the cat.'

I had spent the afternoon creating my most ambitious
disguise ever. Teddy was dressed as a bicycle.

'B-b-but, Uncle, even when there is a cat, the
ch-ch-cheese still gets t-t-taken, d-d-doesn't it?'

'No one is going to steal you, Teddy. I promise.
we are **DANGEROLOGISTS**. we never leave a
DANGEROLOGIST behind.'

We crept along the fence at the edge of the
school so nobody could see us.

'I'm t-t-too scared,' said Teddy.

'Listen, if we can catch the thief, you will get the rest of Liam and everyone else's bikes back. You'll be the hero of the school.'

Teddy swallowed a brave gulp. 'O-O-OK, let's g-g-go.'
I gave him the signal and he sneaked over and nestled into the rack like a parked bicycle, while I looked on from a nearby bush.

We hadn't been waiting long when Spangles appeared. She seemed very surprised to see Teddy, but after a while reversed her back wheels into the rack, like she was pretending to be a bicycle too. A few minutes later, I heard a bell ring. **DING!**

I glanced around, but couldn't see anyone. Then another **DING!**
I realized it was Teddy ringing the bell I had attached to his handlebar-hat. I moved as close to him as I could, while still remaining in the shadows.

'Are you OK, Teddy?' I asked.

'Uncle N-N-Noel, I n-n-need to pee.'

This was tricky. Bikes aren't supposed to pee. If the thief was watching, this would be a big giveaway.

'But you peed before we came out!'

'Well, I n-n-need to go again! I always need to p-p-pee when I'm scared.'

'OK, fine,' I said. There was no point in arguing. 'Sneak off and do it in the bushes.'

Teddy tried to move, but he couldn't.

'Oh, Uncle N-N-Noel! My front wheel is stuck in the bike rack. I c-c-can't g-g-get it out . . .'

Sensing Teddy's worry, Spangles began to meow loudly.
'Here I come!' I said. I ran over, but, as I began to lift him out, suddenly huge spotlights clicked on all around us. A familiar voice came through a loudspeaker.

DO NOT MOVE!
AT LAST, THIEF, WE
HAVE YOU
SURROUNDED!'

It was Jane the policewoman. With her was Springy
Staples and five other officers.

'**NO!**' I said. 'I'm here to catch the thief too!'

'That's what they always say, Zone. Raise your hands
   where we can see them. Keep them away from that bike.'

'But look,' I said. 'This is Teddy, my nephew.'

   Teddy stood up and waved. Nothing like a fright from
   local law enforcement to make your pee suddenly
   disappear.

'And that is the worst part of all,' said Jane. 'That
   you would involve an innocent child in your criminal
   activities. Shame on you, Zone. Somebody take the
   boy home. This man is coming down to the station.'

A Level 5 **DANGEROLOGIST** should try to remain as calm as possible. In every situation you need to ask yourself, what is the **LEAST DANGEROUS** course of action I could take at this time?

But sometimes — very occasionally — you shouldn't stay calm. And one of those times is when lots of people are pointing lights at you in the middle of the night. And also those people want to send you to prison.

At times like these, you should forget all of your **DANGEROLOGY TRAINING** and **run**

away

as

fast

as

you

can.

I have written a poem. This one is entitled:

WANTED

by Docter Noel Zone

I am a wanted criminal,
I am hiding in a tree.
It's not supposed to be like this
For a Level 5 **DOCTER OF DANGEROLOGY.**

Maybe I'll never get home,
In this tree I'll have to settle.
Goodbye Jane, goodbye Teddy,
Goodbye **DANGERZONE,** goodbye Gretel.

Thank you.

NOTE: If you need it, please take a moment to stop crying after that incredible poem.

DANGERBOOTS are surprisingly fast in a chase situation.
I didn't have a plan or an idea where I was going, but
soon found myself in the little wooded area beside the
sports field.

Now, you already know my feelings about trees, but this
was a moment to get over those feelings — or, rather,
climb up them. I found the biggest tree with the thickest,
greenest, best-for-hiding leafy branches and went up it
as fast as I could, as high as I could. And I stayed there
for the night.

At some point I must have dozed off because when I
woke up this morning there was a pigeon sitting on my

DANGER HELMET.

Normally this would have been a **DANGEMERGENCY**, but today has not been a normal day.

'Hello. If you are a glue-poop pigeon, please don't poop on me,' I said to it, 'because it looks like I'll be living up here with you from now on. My name is Noel. I'm going to call you Peter.'

Peter the pigeon seemed to feel sorry for me. He dropped half of the worm he was chomping on to my lap.

'Thank you very much,' I said, pretending to eat it. You don't want to be rude to someone you've just moved in with.

I was really hungry and was starting to think about eating some leaves when a squirrel scampered along the branch next to mine. She was holding a rotten apple.

I was terrified, but did my best to act friendly. 'Hello, squirrel. I'm Docter Noel Zone. I'm living here now. Please don't rob me!'

She seemed very surprised to see me. Maybe she had read the things I'd written about squirrels in my **PORB**, while I was asleep. I thought it was best to apologize, just in case.

'I'm sorry. I'm sure you're not like the other snatchy squirrels, Susie.' She looked like a Susie.

I was camouflaging myself with leaves and branches when I heard a familiar noise.

TOOT

It was the unmistakable sound of a

DAD
(Danger Alerting Device)!

I scanned the area below and
saw Teddy, patrolling in his full
DANGEROLOGY UNIFORM.

I immediately tooted back. **TOOT.**

He couldn't tell where the sound was coming from.

So I tooted twice more — **TOOT, TOOT,** meaning 'LOOK UP'.

But Teddy wasn't aware of this Level 3 **DANGEROLOGY**
DAD-code.

So next I made a sound like a magpie. 'CAW, CAW.'
But this seemed to confuse him even more.

He shouted,

'BIRDY, DO YOU KNOW WHERE MY UNCLE IS?'

Nobody else was around
so I just called down.
'I'm up here in the big tree!'

He ran over and stood underneath me.

'I can't come down,' I explained from the
lowest branch. 'I might be arrested.'

'So how l-l-long are you going to stay there?'

'I don't know, maybe forever. Could you do me a
favour? Could you get me some food? I'm so hungry
and there are only rotten apples and worms up here.'

'I'll bring something with me to sports d-d-day later on!'

'And thanks for coming back for me, Teddy.'

'We are **D-D-DANGEROLOGISTS**,' he said. 'We never
leave a **DANGEROLOGIST** b-b-behind.'

My **DASK** was learning.

SATURDAY, LATE MORNING — A SPORTS DAY TO REMEMBER

From up in the tree I could see everything.

'Maybe you've got the right idea, Susie. Maybe I'll get used to living here.' But, when I looked over at her, she was nibbling on her rotten apple while Peter pulled a worm out of the top of it.

Not long after Teddy's visit, Mr Staples began setting up for sports day. He wheeled out a big loudspeaker with a wireless microphone and put down cones to separate the different areas for the activities.

On the opposite side of the sports field I could see Gretel setting up a refreshments stand.

And, I have to say, she was setting it up better than I've ever seen anyone set anything up.

Soon students in their sports gear began arriving with their whole families. The poor BMX gang all burst into tears when they found that some of their bikes had come back.

When everyone had gathered, Mr Staples started droning out his announcements. He sounded even more boring through a loudspeaker.

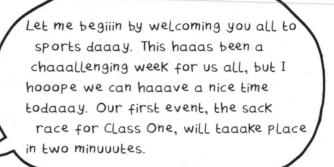

Let me begiiin by welcoming you all to sports daaay. This haaas been a chaaallenging week for us all, but I hooope we can haaave a nice time todaaay. Our first event, the sack race for Class One, will taaake place in two minuuutes.

That was Teddy's class!

This was my first ever sports day and I'd never heard of a 'sack race'. How would they get sacks to race? Maybe pull them along with string? Or wait for the wind to blow them the length of the track?

Then I saw the **AWFUL** and **DANGEROUS** truth.

The competitors were standing **INSIDE** their sacks

AND THEN TRYING TO BOUNCE ALONG FASTER THAN EACH OTHER?

No, no, no, no, no. I did not like this.

Suddenly being stuck up here was torture – I could see all of this **DANGER** but couldn't **DO ANYTHING** about it.

Some events like the tug o' war seemed safe at first.
Two teams holding a piece of rope — nothing wrong with
that. But then Springy Staples said '**GO**' and

IT TURNED INTO ONE OF THE MOST
DANGEROUS THINGS I'VE EVER SEEN.

I MEAN, WHAT IF THE ROPE BROKE?

OR IF IT WAS A SNAKE?

WHAT IF ONE OF THE CONTESTANTS
WAS A VERY STRONG APE?

OR IF A GIANT EAGLE SWOOPED
DOWN AND PICKED UP THE ROPE?

I noticed there was some confusion
going on underneath me because
Springy couldn't find his microphone.
   He had a group of teachers and
students searching for it.

'Everything is going missing in this school, Susie,'
I said. 'Susie . . . Susie? Oh, there you are.'

She was making her way back up the tree trunk,
but this time she wasn't carrying an apple —
it was too big and silver and microphoney . . .

SUSIE HAD STOLEN MR STAPLES'
MICROPHONE!

Below us, Springy was standing on a table, yelling details of the next event.

'PLEASE ASSEMBLE FOR
CLASS FIVE'S THREE-LEGGED RACE.'

At first I thought a three-legged race sounded a lot safer than a two-legged one — everyone with their extra leg, maybe on a walking stick, so they would be even less likely to fall over . . .

But then I saw Katherine and Millicent practising at the side of the track, doing a wobbly sprint with two of their legs tied together and I couldn't stop myself. I grabbed the microphone from Susie and did my best Springy impersonation.

In a chaaange to the programme, the three-legged raaace is now renamed 'the no-legged raaace' and the competitors have to lie on the ground and see who can go to sleep first.

NOEL

And do you know what? Everyone did exactly what the announcement told them to do. They all lay down in their lanes and tried their hardest to snooze.

Below me, Mr Staples was looking utterly baffled. He had no idea where this voice was coming from.

After five minutes nobody was asleep, so I declared it a draw.

'Congratulaaations! You're all in joint first plaaace,' I said. And they all seemed absolutely delighted.

I was determined to change this from an ordinary sports day to

A Sports Day WAFOS

(With A Focus On Safety).

The sack raaace for Class Four that is about to take place will also have a slight chaaange of ruuules. The competitors have to waaalk around the sports field, picking up any liiitter or leaves and putting them in their saaacks. The winner is the person who has gaaathered the most.

I turned the egg-and-spoon race into the 'hold-a-cabbage-in-your-hands-and-walk-very-carefully walk', and all of the running races became 'backwards crawling'.

I changed the welly-boot-throwing to 'see how quickly you can put on and take off the **DANGERBOOT**'.

'Dangerbooots? **CAAABBAGES?**' Staples screamed out below me. 'Wait a second! I know who says those things . . .

ZOOOONE! where are you? I knooow you are behind this.'

Only one person knew where I was. And he had remembered to bring me some food, but, being Teddy, he had got a little too enthusiastic. He suddenly appeared on my branch, beside me.

'H-H-Hello, Uncle Noel!'

'How did you get up here? I hope nobody saw you. Oh, Teddy, this is much too dangerous!'

'But you're up h-h-here, Uncle! And you always say that you're the g-g-greatest **DANGEROLOGIST** in the w-w-world!'

But all other thoughts vanished when Teddy reached into his backpack and presented me with one of Gretel's cabbages.

I shoved it into my face and ate half of it right then.

'This must be the s-s-safest s-s-sports day ever,' Teddy said, as we watched the competitors in the 50-metre hurdles crawl backwards under their hurdles.

I was about to agree, but then I saw Roxanne the zookeeper coming through the school gates. Uh-oh. She was holding a lead — a very long lead. And it seemed to be going upwards. And upwards.

And upwards. With a **VERY** familiar and annoying face on the end of it: **NOEL THE GIRAFFE.**

I could hear Springy yell out, 'AS PART OF THE ZOO'S
OUTREACH PROGRAMME, THEY HAVE SENT US A
SPECIAL GUEST. EVERYBODY WELCOME THEIR
NEWEST GIRAFFE, NO—'

He couldn't bring himself to even say my name.

'THEIR NEWEST GIRAFFE, NEAL!'

There was a round of applause and
everyone rushed over to say hello.

'Stay away from the giraffe!' I announced on the microphone. 'Seriously, he could go **CRAZY** at any moment. Look at those weird ping-pong-ball eyes.'

But nobody was listening to my announcements any more. They wanted to get a photograph with him, but Noel the giraffe was hungry and was trying to eat the ivy from the front of the school. Then I saw Katherine point Roxanne towards my clump of trees.

'Oh no. Don't come over here!'

Soon Noel was munching on the apple tree next door,
or whatever you say when you live in a tree.
Next tree, I suppose.

'If we stay really quiet, Noel might just go away,'
I tried to whisper to Teddy, Peter and Susie, but forgot
that the microphone was still on. And when Noel heard
my voice he started to bounce around.

Peter flapped up into the sky and that was the only
clue Noel needed. He thrust his big stupid head into the
place in the tree where Peter had been, and, once again,
we came face to face.

HUNDRED AND NOELTY-FOUR

'Please stay calm, Noel!' I pleaded with him. 'Don't give me away, or I'll have to go to prison! That's like the zoo but with even less space.'

'Have t-t-this —' said Teddy, giving him the second half of my cabbage.

Not surprisingly, Noel had never tasted anything as delicious as Gretel's cabbage. Now, the two Noels had one more thing in common.

While he munched, I tried to explain my predicament to him. 'Everyone thinks I've been taking the bicycles from over there.'

As I pointed towards the school, I spotted somebody
familiar. It was Mrs Waddock, probably going in to
work on her noisy organ again. Oh, now she was
looking at the bikes. Probably just checking to see if
they were safe. Then I saw her stop at one — it was
Gretel's, with the big cabbage basket on the front.
She looked around for a moment, then took some keys from
her pocket. Next she started trying different ones in
Gretel's lock . . . It took a second for me to realize
what I was seeing . . . **MRS WADDOCK WAS THE BIKE THIEF!**

'**LOOK!**' I pointed it out to Teddy.

'**W-W-WHOA!**' he said.

But it would take too long to climb down and run after her.
She'd have escaped by then.

'F-f-follow me, Uncle!'

Teddy reached out, as if to hug Noel the giraffe, but
then he slid down his neck like it was a fire-fighter's pole.

'WHAT ARE YOU DOING?'

I had no option but to follow my nephew.

Next thing, we were both sitting on Noel the giraffe's back,
facing the wrong direction.

I pointed backwards, towards Mrs Waddock, and said,

'FOLLOW THAT THIEF, NOEL.'

The whole thing happened so quickly and unexpectedly that Noel the giraffe yanked the lead out of Roxanne the zookeeper's hand, and the two Noels and one Teddy took off after Mrs Waddock.

When she saw us coming, she jumped on Gretel's bike and tried to pedal away.

'STOP! T-T-THIEF!' shouted Teddy.

By now, everyone at sports day had seen what was going on.

'I see Captain Dingbat is riding a giraffe backwards,'
said Sunglasses.

'Nothing surprises me about that guy,' added Hood.

'Wait! That's Teddy on there too!' said Hat.

'Do we all get to ride the giraffe?' asked Spike.

The others ignored him and shouted,

'GO ON, TEDDY!' as loud as they could.

We chased Mrs Waddock once round the sports track and
everyone cheered as we passed.

We were gaining on her.

Then she turned and cycled straight through the main door into the school.

'She's heading for the music room!' said Teddy.

'**FOLLOW HER, NOEL!**' I said.

Noel the giraffe ducked to get in through the main door and as we clomped along the corridor Mrs Waddock seemed to be running out of energy. Soon we had drawn level with her and Noel began licking her face with his enormous football-sock tongue.

'**AAAARRRRGH!**' she bleated. 'I'm covered in giraffe goo!'

As we neared the end of the corridor, I noticed Spangles straight ahead. She had pawed open the door of the paper cupboard — maybe the lock was **MUCH** easier to open than I had thought. Noel the giraffe skidded to a halt, but Mrs Waddock freewheeled into the cupboard where her journey came to an abrupt end with her head stuck in the photocopier.

Mr Staples was first on the scene. He had tears of joy in his eyes. 'You've dooone it, Zone and Teddy! You've saaaved the daaay!'

Teddy had the first question. 'What have you d-d-done with the r-r-rest of our bikes, Mrs Waddock?'

'I was using the parts to build my organ,' she said as photocopies of her mean face filled the out-tray.

Teddy ran into the music room and opened the big wooden shutters that covered the keyboard. Behind it, hundreds of bicycle parts had been reused as organ components — handlebars as pipes, wheels as pulleys and rows of bicycle bells being hit by the handle of Mr Staples' Segway.

'Teddy, you're a hero!' said Sunglasses, and everyone erupted in applause.

'Thank you for getting our bikes back, Teddy and Captain Dingbat!' said Hood and Hat.

'Is the photocopier OK?' asked Spike.

As the kids ran inside and began to take the organ apart, Jane the policewoman arrived and put handcuffs on Mrs Waddock. 'We wouldn't have caught her without your help, Noel. Thank you.'

'Oh, that's OK,' I said. 'I was just doing my job as a **DANGEROLOGIST.** And sometimes you get stuck in a **DORK** or have to ride a giraffe backwards. But I'm definitely not **DANGEROUS.**'

'Please don't get into any trouble around here again, Doctor,' she said.

'I'll do my very best! Oh, and it's actually Doct**ER** . . .'

But Jane was already leading Mrs Waddock back down the corridor towards the police car.

'Thank you so much for saving my bicycle,' Gretel said as I poured her a cup of not-too-warm cabbage tea. 'I thought you were very brave.'

I blushed slightly. 'Oh, it was nothing.'

'And it was so ingenious to use the tree as a lookout tower to catch the thief. How long would you have waited up there?'

'As long as it took, Gretel. As long as it took.'

'What if it had taken weeks? How would you have survived?'

'On these, of course,' I said, reaching down for the cabbage with a bow round it that she had given me as a thank-you gift. But the cabbage was gone.
'Where is it?' I said.

'This tea is delicious, Noel,' she said, having another sip.

I went to drink mine, but my cup was almost empty.
'Hey! What is going on?'

'Oh, and thanks again for my helmet,' she said.
'It's perfect for cycling.'

'Oh, yes. Everyone should have a good **DANGER HELMET.**'
And, as I said that, I suddenly felt mine being lifted off my head with a loud slurping sound.

By the time I looked up, Noel the giraffe had flipped
my helmet on to his head and was eating my cabbage,
which he had stolen off the table.

As he leaned in to drink the rest of my cabbage tea,
Gretel said, 'I think you've got a new friend. Do you
mind if I call in sometimes to say hello to him?'

I **REALLY** liked that idea. 'Not at all, Gretel.
Please call in **ANY** time.'

I looked up at Noel as cabbage bits snowed down on us.
'Thank you, Noel the giraffe,' I thought to myself.
'Maybe we Noels should be friends after all.'

WAIT!

This book is not finished yet.

I said you would be a qualified Level 3 **FOD**
(**F**ull-**O**n **D**angerologist) if you got to the end.

Well, you are **NOT QUITE AT THE END.**

Similar to the **DROST** you had to complete to **START**
this book, in order to **FINISH** it you have to pass the
Level 3 **DETBAFOD** (**D**angerology **E**xamination **T**o **B**ecome
A Full-**O**n **D**angerologist). You will be tested on everything
you have learned in this book.

Thank you.

NOTE: If you don't get all of the questions correct in the **DETBAFOD**, I'm afraid you will have to go back and read this **ENTIRE** book again. And you're not allowed to read another book till you get them all right.

I'm sorry, but these are the rules.

NOTE 2: I know these are the rules because I made up the rules myself.

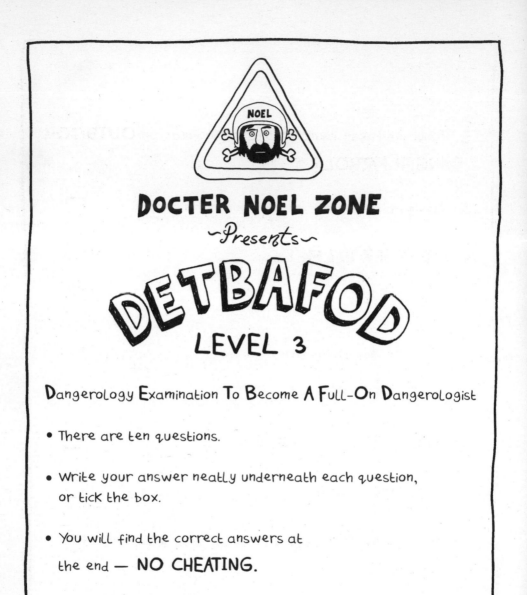

DOCTER NOEL ZONE

~Presents~

DETBAFOD

LEVEL 3

Dangerology Examination To Become A Full-On Dangerologist

- There are ten questions.

- Write your answer neatly underneath each question, or tick the box.

- You will find the correct answers at the end — **NO CHEATING.**

GOOD LUCK, Level 3 PODs!

1. Which of these items is suitable to wear on **OUTDOOR DANGER PATROL?**

(a) Flip-flops on fire ☐

(b) A **DANGER HELMET** cone ☐

(c) Rollerblades ☐

2. What does **DORK** stand for?

(a) **D**o **O**nly **R**oundhouse **K**icks ☐

(b) **D**ogs **O**bserve **R**oad **K**ill ☐

(c) **D**anger **O**bservation **R**econnaissance **K**art ☐

3. What do ghosts smell like?

(a) Parp donkeys ☐

(b) Gross old shoes ☐

(c) Cabbages ☐

4. Which of these seasons sees the most **ALLEAFGATOR** attacks?

(a) Autumn ☐

(b) Spring ☐

(c) The rugby season ☐

5. Which object is the safest to sit on?

(a) A beanbag ☐

(b) A bicycle ☐

(c) A giraffe ☐

6. Which of these places is the best to store your **PORB**?

(a) In a giant's mouth ☐

(b) In the basket of a bicycle ☐

(c) Between two slices of bread ☐

7. How do you scare away a **CLASSROOM CHAMELEON?**

(a) With a **RAD HORN** ☐

(b) With garlic ☐

(c) With some particularly difficult fractions homework ☐

8. Which of these is the **SAFEST** title for a play?

(a) 'Romeo and Juliet and a Trapeze' ☐

(b) 'Two People on Beanbags Staring at a Bin' ☐

(c) 'Smashy, Smashy, Boom, Boom' ☐

NOEL. Which of these is the **SAFEST ATHLETICS EVENT?**

(a) Hedgehog-Kangaroo wrestling ☐

(b) Crawling (slowly) backwards **UNDER** hurdles ☐

(c) High-speed tree-climbing ☐

10. What is the best thing to have for lunch every day?

(a) Cabbage soup ☐

(b) Cabbage soup ☐

(c) Cabbage soup ☐

ANSWERS TO DEBTAFOD
(LEVEL 3)

1. (b) A **DANGER HELMET** cone adds a **SNAZZY** and **SAFE** element to every outfit.

2. (c) **D**anger **O**bservation **R**econnaissance **K**art

3. (b) Gross old shoes. Yuck. Just when you thought ghosts couldn't be any more yucky and annoying.

4. (a) **ALLEAFGATORS** attack in autumn when there are lots of fallen leaves for them to hide under.

5. (a) A beanbag, of course! Just make sure it is a beanbag and not a sleepy sea lion.

6. (c) The best place to store your **PORB** is between two slices of bread. **DON'T EAT IT, THOUGH!**

7. (c) **CLASSROOM CHAMELEONS** are scared of maths. In fact that's why we've put some sums on the opposite page. You can cut out the page to get rid of any

CLASSROOM CHAMELEONS.

8. (b) 'Two People on Beanbags Staring at a Bin' is the safest title for a play. If they are ever staged,

PLEASE DO NOT GO TO SEE THESE OTHER PLAYS.

NOEL. (b) Crawling (slowly) backwards **UNDER** hurdles is the safest athletics event. Also, the winner in this race is the person who comes **LAST.**

10. I will accept **(a), (b)** or **(c)** as the correct answer here.

x74

6)52

$\times 800$

x23

$\begin{array}{r} 39 \\ \times 21 \\ \hline \end{array}$

8)340 =

$\begin{array}{r} 56 \\ \times 20 \\ \hline \end{array}$

$\begin{array}{r} 10 \\ \times 23 \\ \hline \end{array}$

2)88

$\begin{array}{r} 10 \\ \times 62 \\ \hline \end{array}$

$\begin{array}{r} 16 \\ \times 74 \\ \hline \end{array}$

8)340 =

$\begin{array}{r} 10 \\ \times 62 \\ \hline \end{array}$

$\begin{array}{r} 56 \\ \times 20 \\ \hline \end{array}$

6)528 =

$\begin{array}{r} 56 \\ \times 20 \\ \hline \end{array}$

6)528

8)340 =

$\begin{array}{r} 39 \\ \times 21 \\ \hline \end{array}$

x4

GO AWAY, CLASSROOM CHAMELEON!

6)528 =

$\begin{array}{r} 39 \\ \times 21 \\ \hline \end{array}$

$\begin{array}{r} 10 \\ \times 62 \\ \hline \end{array}$

8)340 =

$\begin{array}{r} 16 \\ \times 74 \\ \hline \end{array}$

$\begin{array}{r} 39 \\ \times 21 \\ \hline \end{array}$

8)340 =

$\begin{array}{r} 39 \\ \times 21 \\ \hline \end{array}$

$\begin{array}{r} 56 \\ \times 20 \\ \hline \end{array}$

6)528 =

$\begin{array}{r} 56 \\ \times 20 \\ \hline \end{array}$

$\begin{array}{r} 10 \\ \times 62 \\ \hline \end{array}$

5)3

$\begin{array}{r} 45 \\ \times 800 \\ \hline \end{array}$

8)340 =

$\begin{array}{r} 56 \\ \times 20 \\ \hline \end{array}$

$\begin{array}{r} 39 \\ \times 21 \\ \hline \end{array}$

2)88 =

9)864

16

45

×74

6)528

×800

×23

39
21

8)340 =

10
×62

56
×20

16
×74

10
×23

2)88 =

56
20

6)528 =

8)340 =

56
×20

10
×62

340 =

6)528 =

39
×21

57
×47

GO AWAY,
CLASSROOM
CHAMELEON!

528 =

39
×21

10
×62

8)340 =

16
×74

39
×21

8)340 =

39
21

56
×20

6)528 =

56
×20

5)375

10
×62

+5
800

8)340 =

56
×20

10
×62

39
×21

2)88 =

9)864 =

16

If you got all of the answers correct,

PLEASE TURN TO THE NEXT PAGE.

If you didn't, **DO NOT TURN OVER!**
Please go back to the start and begin this book again.

DOD (DIPLOMA OF DANGEROLOGY) Level 3

THIS IS TO CERTIFY THAT

DOCTER...

(sign your name here)

has reached an excellent level of knowledge in

AAAAaAAA, TTTFADIES and **GENERAL DANGEROLOGY**

and is no longer a **LEVEL 3 POD,** but now a **LEVEL 3 FOD**.

You can now pilot your own **DORK** – but please be careful of hills.

And remember at all times that

DANGER REALLY IS EVERYWHERE

Docter Noel Zone

DOCTER NOEL ZONE (Level 5 DANGEROLOGIST)

DANGER

REALLY IS

EVERYWHERE

was written with
the help of my neighbours

DAVID O'DOHERTY (words)
and CHRIS JUDGE (pictures)

David ⟶

 ⟵ Chris

David O'Doherty is a comedian, writer and regular guest on television shows such as *QI*, *Have I Got News For You* and *Would I Lie To You?* He has written two theatre shows for children, including one where he fixed their bicycles live on stage.

Chris Judge is the award-winning author/illustrator of *The Lonely Beast* and a number of other picture books for children. His recent work includes Roddy Doyle's novel *Brilliant* and a week spent in a cafe where he painted breadboards with pictures of animals that may never have existed.

They met when Chris was in a band and David used to come and watch.
They both live in Dublin.